A Land of
Heart's Desire

THE SEVENTH CHILD SERIES

JOY PENNOCK GAGE

A Land of Heart's Desire
Book 1

Lee William's Quest
Book 2

A Waiting Legacy
Book 3

A Land of Heart's Desire

Joy Pennock Gage

Harold Shaw Publishers
Wheaton, Illinois

ISBN 0-87788-485-4

Cover design by Ron Kadrmas

Cover illustration © 1991 by Kevin Beilfuss

Library of Congress Cataloging-in-Publication Data

Gage, Joy P.
    A land of heart's desire / Joy Pennock Gage.
        p.   cm. — (The seventh child series / Joy Pennock Gage ; bk. 1)
    ISBN 0-87788-485-4
    I. Title. II. Series: Gage, Joy P. Seventh child series ; bk. 1.
    PS3557.A329L3 1991
    813'.54—dc20   91-8618
                                         CIP

---

00 99 98 97 96 95 94 93 92 91
10 9 8 7 6 5 4 3 2 1

*To the descendants
of the real Grandma MaryAnn,
with whom I happily share
a common bloodline*

CONTENTS

CHAPTER ONE

Indiana, 1854

———— ∽ ————

ad it not been for William John's horse, MaryAnn Brean Chidester might have lived all her days in Indiana. If William John hadn't tracked that stolen horse clean into Missouri and found him under a great oak tree on Solomon's Ridge, they might not be moving away from her home—the home where MaryAnn had grown up and where she and William John had raised their family.

And maybe, just maybe, if William John hadn't been so morbid about the school ruckus he wouldn't have bothered to go so far to find that horse and somehow in the finding end up agreeing to open a school on Dogwood Creek in the Missouri hills.

But William John *had* followed his stolen horse to Dogwood Creek, and he *had* made a promise. It was done and MaryAnn couldn't bring herself to stand against William John's plans.

How could she? After all, she had been with him that cold March night at the new schoolhouse, when William John sat silent, red-faced, and fairly bursting with anger. She had seen him jump up, stretching his long lanky frame to full

1

height before he spoke. And then, running his fingers through his unruly brown hair, he had argued that White Creek needed a free school. MaryAnn could see his jumper bobbing with his quick hard breaths when he repeated what he'd already said a dozen times and more: "It's a crime against democracy to let children grow up in ignorance!"

As usual, Ed Peevey was the first to respond, jumping up and hollering, "Then let the parents educate their own young'uns. The missus and me, we don't hold to payin' for educatin' other people's brats!"

After that display of pigheaded ignorance, William John said no more. He sat straight and silent on the bench beside MaryAnn, listening intently to Peevey's outburst and shaking his head all the while. When Peevey had finished, William John turned to MaryAnn, his lips parted as if to speak. Then, drawing a deep breath, he shrugged helplessly and turned away again. In that brief glance MaryAnn saw the first signs of defeat in her husband's usually bright eyes.

Some had allowed that Ed Peevey was right. A few timidly disagreed. But the sum of the matter was that there was no money to run a free school, so the newly built school was closed just two months after it had opened.

MaryAnn and William John left the meeting in silence. The moon had disappeared behind a cloud, leaving the road shrouded in darkness. They walked the two miles home, accompanied only by the sound of the lantern softly squeaking on its bail and the crunch of the still-frozen ground under their feet.

They were at their gate before William John spoke a word. In the shadowy lantern light she had seen his finely chiseled jaws tighten as he demanded through clenched teeth, "Mary-Ann, isn't there anyone in the whole of Indiana that can see we are becoming the most illiterate state in the Union? Can't somebody do something about it?"

She ignored his question for a moment, hoping he would find the answer himself. She waited until they were inside the house and William John had set the lantern down. Then she responded, "There's at least one, William John. *You* see it, and you can do somethin'."

"I can't!" His reply was sharp. "I've tried too many years. Caleb Mills has been fighting this same fight for twenty years or more—ever since he came to Indiana. If an instructor at Wabash College can't convince folks to fund public schools, what can I do?" William John flung his hands wide in disgust.

"Don't give up now," MaryAnn pleaded with her husband.

But William John did give up. She could see it in his eyes the next morning. He had left their bed in the middle of the night—walking off his anger in the south pasture she was sure. When he came in from his morning chores, she could see that the anger was gone. But the observation gave her no relief. Instead, a moment of fear gripped her heart as she noted that along with the anger, something else had gone out of William John.

For a week afterward he had gone about saying nothing, always off somewhere in his mind. For the first few days, MaryAnn chafed with anger at those who had allowed the school to close. Then her anger gave way to worry over her husband, for it was obvious that more than a school had been lost. William John looked like a man who had lost his very last dream.

And then someone stole William John's horse.

MaryAnn remembered the morning clearly. It was the tenth of March—over a month ago now—when William John came in from the barn before the biscuits were even baked, calling to her without stopping to hang up his hat, "My horse is gone! Someone stole my horse in the night. Pack me a grubsack, MaryAnn. I'm going to track that thief, and I'll not be back without my horse!"

To MaryAnn, William John seemed almost glad that the horse was gone, as though it gave him an excuse to pursue something new. A glow of excitement shone in his dark brown eyes. It was a look she had not seen for a long while, and a hint of excitement gripped her own heart as she watched her husband make hurried preparations to leave.

There's no explainin' him, she mused. *What a lost school took away, a lost horse has put back!* For three weeks she carried in her mind the vision of William John riding away after his horse. In the lonely hours of the night, she contented herself with the knowledge that the look in his eye was that of a man who hadn't given up. And she wondered what might happen when he returned.

The look was still there, even brighter, when he came home a week ago—leading his horse behind—full of plans to move to Missouri. He came back a man who had discovered he could still dream. Who was MaryAnn to stand in his way?

CHAPTER TWO

A Dream for Everyone?

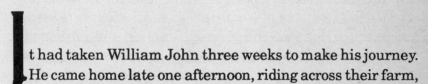

It had taken William John three weeks to make his journey. He came home late one afternoon, riding across their farm, his brown hair blowing as he waved his hat at the house. MaryAnn felt a quick wave of joy and relief rush over her at the sight of her husband. She hurried to the barnlot to meet him. They walked back to the house, arm in arm.

She pressed his arm more tightly than usual, but said nothing of the anxiety she had felt during his absence. Her pioneer mother had embedded in MaryAnn's thinking that women must be strong—that men had enough to worry about with crops and weather and stock and that a woman should be careful not to add to those burdens. Characteristically now, she said nothing of what was in her heart. Instead she asked matter-of-factly, "How far did you have to go?"

"We went clean over into Missouri."

"We?"

"Lucy's pa went along."

"Well, I s'pose that even Jubal Tate would make good company on such a journey."

5

"More than good company. Most likely I'd never have found my horse without Jubal. Nobody outsmarts him in the woods. I can see now why our son thinks so highly of his father-in-law."

He slipped his hand under her elbow and guided her around a mudhole in the path as he spoke.

MaryAnn tried not to show her surprise at William John's admiration of this Tennessee woodsman who had given his daughter all the necessities but not one day of book learning. Jubal's own mother had taught Lucy everything she needed to know about keeping a house. Lucy had earned a reputation for both her baking and her quilting long before she married Lee William, the seventh son of MaryAnn and William John. From the first, William John found much to admire in his new daughter-in-law, but he had never taken to loud-mouthed Jubal Tate before. MaryAnn found the sudden change curious, but she didn't press the matter.

"I'm glad you had company, William John," she said.

"Indeed! It seemed mighty lonely coming home without him."

"You came home without him!" MaryAnn exclaimed. "Is he sick? Oh, I hope not. That would be hard for Lucy, her bein' in the family way and all."

"No, no. He's not sick." Then William John paused for so long that MaryAnn turned her head towards him.

"He decided to stay in Missouri," William John said. "He contracted with a lumber company to cut timber and he's already started building himself a cabin. I expect it's up by now."

He looked directly at MaryAnn's upturned face as he continued. "MaryAnn, I want to move to Missouri."

Her blue-black eyes widened in disbelief.

6

They were at the kitchen door. MaryAnn stopped still, gripped by a fear she could neither explain nor put a name to. She stared at her husband. "Move to Missouri!" she exclaimed. "You haven't even set foot inside your home yet and you're already talkin' about movin'?"

William John opened the door and motioned for MaryAnn to enter. "That's just it. I can set foot in the door and even sit here at the table, but this isn't my home, and it never will be. This was your parents' home, and now it's your brother's."

MaryAnn felt a tightening about her heart. *What did he mean—"this isn't my home, and it never will be"?* Of course this was their home. Her own orphaned father had built it with his grandfather. She had been born in this very house—the seventh child of her German immigrant mother. And she and William John had been married here on her sixteenth birthday by a circuit preacher who came regularly to White Creek. It was here she had given birth to their seven sons, here she had grieved at the deathbeds of two, here she had stood at the doorway and waved good-bye to three others. How could he say, "this isn't my home"?

As for her brother owning the house, it was true that her father had left the farm to George. But it was his intention that this massive home would be shared with William John and MaryAnn. And why not? The Brean log house had always been the talk of White Creek because it had more rooms than any log house around. There were five bedrooms upstairs, two downstairs, a parlor, and a kitchen large enough to accommodate a dozen or more people at one meal.

MaryAnn snapped out of her musing. "There's plenty room for all of us," she protested. "It's not like George had married and had a family of his own. It's our home as long as we need it."

She sat down at the table across from William John, holding her hands tightly in her lap to keep them from trembling. Giving him no time to respond, she continued, "I don't rightly see how you can say this isn't your home. You've lived here most of your life—since before we married, when you came lookin' for a temporary job before your first school term."

MaryAnn's eyes grew misty at the memory of William John's coming to the Brean home for the first time. He had ridden from the village with George in George's fancy Irish jaunting cart. From that first meeting, she knew she would marry William John Chidester one day. He had stayed that summer, then moved away for the school term. They married the next summer and had made their home in the Brean house ever since.

Not once in all those years had it crossed her mind that her husband might one day want to leave this home. Keeping her head down so William John would not see the mist in her eyes, she said very quietly, "It's been your home for a long time, William John."

"I know that," he said gently. "But it's not enough, Mary-Ann. A man wants a place of his own—a place he can leave to his own children." And then, as if trying to ward off MaryAnn's next protest, William John continued, "Remember, we already have three sons in Missouri, not to speak of your two half brothers. I found my horse on Dogwood Creek— three days ride from Tipton. I know that's still a long ways but it's a sight closer than we are now. Might be we could see family more often."

MaryAnn was disarmed by the fervency in his voice. His fine angular face seemed younger than his forty-eight years.

His eyes danced with excitement. She wanted to protest further, but the words caught in her throat. She listened silently as William John poured out his dreams about Dogwood Creek.

Once started, it was as if he couldn't keep still. He grabbed her hand and squeezed it as he described what he had seen. "It's a beautiful valley—a 'holler,' they call it. It's right on the edge of the Ozarks. You can get land cheap from the lumber company, work up the timber and farm on the side. And one of the families promised to talk to the other families about starting a school—"

"They don't have a school?" MaryAnn interrupted.

"No, they've never had a teacher on Dogwood Creek before," he replied enthusiastically.

She knew then that this was the heart of the matter for her husband.

"Sounds primitive, William John. And how do you expect to farm and cut timber and teach school?"

His response was quick. "I've thought about that. I was figuring the boys might go along. Lucy's pa sent word that Lee William and Lucy could live with him, temporary-like and Lee William could help him in the timber this year when we're not needing him."

"But Lucy's expectin'! That's a long trip for her." MaryAnn jumped up and hurried to the cookstove. She stirred the beans simmering in their pot and added more water from the kettle.

"All the more reason why we have to hurry. We can get settled before her time comes." William John waited for MaryAnn to rejoin him before continuing. A small frown creased his brow and he scratched the slight stubble on his chin. "I am a mite worried about your brother, though, it being the first year since your pa died. Our moving might leave George with more work than he can handle."

"It's not George I worry about. There's young men around here lookin' for work. And I s'pose Lee William and Lucy would be happy to stake out some land of their own. It's Russell Brean I'm worried about."

Her husband was silent for a moment at the mention of their fourth son who was now twenty-six. "You worry about him too much, MaryAnn," William John said gently. "Fact is, you worry more about him than all your other sons put together. Maybe it's because you gave him the Brean family name and you expect him to do all the things your pa did. You got to remember that he's Russell Brean Chidester and he might want to do things different. I know he acts hotheaded sometimes but life's not been easy for him with that useless arm."

"I can't see that it's hindered him any," MaryAnn replied, shrugging. "He's made a right good hand on the farm."

"Of course he has. Don't you see, he's set out to prove he can do anything a man with two good arms can do. Trying to prove himself is the only thing that's kept him on this farm. Truth to tell, he can't abide farming."

MaryAnn looked down at her hands, tightly gripped in her lap once more. She spoke softly. "The way I see it, William John, our son can't abide us most of the time. You said you was figurin' on the boys goin' along. Does that mean you expect Russell to go, too?"

"I'll need all the help I can get this season, and I'm hoping he'll go, but it's his decision. Russell's a man. He can come with us or he can work out something with George. No reason why he can't continue to live here with your brother. I'll not tell him what to do, one way or the other."

"He does take to George," MaryAnn agreed. "I expect he'd have been long gone before this if it hadn't been for his Uncle George."

MaryAnn grew pensive, remembering the many times she and William John had sat at this very table discussing Russell's relationship with his uncle. George had always had a special way with the boy. It was George who had forced MaryAnn and William John to stand back and let their son struggle. "He won't always have somebody around to tie his shoes or button his jumper," George had declared. "He has to learn to do things for himself." William John had seen the wisdom of George's words at once. And MaryAnn had agreed but she allowed that it was not easy for a mother to stand by while a crippled child tried to fend for himself. Even now she found herself wanting to do for Russell.

Ignoring both her remark and her mood, William John continued his enthusiastic description of his plans. Neither of them heard the door open and shut as Russell himself entered the room. Slightly under six foot, he had the stocky build of his grandfather Brean. In addition, he had the Brean's raven-black hair and eyes. They were stormy now as he stood silently, listening to the conversation. Slowly, he reached his right hand across his chest and began to tug at his left arm, which hung limp in its sleeve.

At the table William John looked at his wife intently. "MaryAnn, I think it's time Russell left off farming and found something else to do. I do need him this year, but after that—well, I have an idea that—"

"I'll just wager you do at that, Pa!" Russell exploded.

Startled, MaryAnn looked up to see her son standing near the door, his mouth curled in sarcasm. *He's angry as a hornet,* she thought, seeing him pull at his left arm.

William John ignored his son's obvious anger. Jumping to his feet, he walked quickly to Russell and extended his hand in greeting. "We didn't hear you come in, Son. How long you been standing there?"

"Long enough." For a moment Russell looked at William John's outstretched hand. But he didn't extend his own. Instead he clamped it hard on his left arm. Then, giving the withered limb a final jerk, he turned from his father and stomped out of the house.

———

Long experience had taught MaryAnn that it would do no good to go after Russell. She felt the familiar stab of pain that came with the memory of the double tragedies that had marked the life of her fourth born. He had been only five years old the winter the fever had come to White Creek and raged through every home for miles around. Russell had escaped the fever but not the pain of it, for his two younger brothers had died. At the burying, and for days afterward, he had stood silent as a stone, asking no questions, saying nothing.

And then the accident happened.

Folks all around had begun to rest easier—there had been no new graves in over three weeks—when Russell Brean Chidester fell from a runaway wagon. As he lay sprawled beside the wagon rut, unable to move, the massive rear wheel rolled over his left arm. By the time William John reined in the team, the boy's screams had ceased. His whitened face was still marked with pain but he lay limp and silent.

At the house MaryAnn watched in terror as her husband carried their young son from the wagon. William John took time only to lay the child on the bed before he hurried away to fetch the doctor. He blurted out scanty details as he ran from the room.

Standing alone beside the motionless child, MaryAnn was suddenly overcome by the realization of what might have been. *What if the wagon had run over his head?* she questioned. She sank beside the bed and buried her head in the coverlet. Quietly, hoping not to disturb the boy, she sobbed. And when she was done she could not tell if she cried for her sons so recently buried, or for the pain of young Russell or for the horror of what he had escaped. As she stood and wiped her tears on her apron, she felt relief that only an arm had been injured.

The doctor was quick to agree with MaryAnn. Gently he examined the arm, shaking his head all the while. "He's a lucky boy," he declared. "It's a simple break. He'll be as good as new in no time."

But as the days passed, a fever set in. Russell woke up morning after morning asking, "Where's my arm, Mama? I can't feel my arm anymore." Reluctantly the doctor concluded that something had been separated in the shoulder area. "There's been some kind of nerve damage, I'll wager, but I don't recollect seeing anything in my medical books about this kind of injury." Out of the boy's hearing, he said that if Russell lived, he might never have use of his arm again.

Once again all of White Creek kept vigil while one of their young lay close to death. They waited for six long weeks and when Russell Chidester was well again they clucked their tongues at the arm that hung limp and useless at his side.

It had been a bitter time for MaryAnn. She had wanted to shake her fist at the Almighty who would spare a son from the fever only to cripple him in an accident.

In the privacy of their bedroom, MaryAnn spilled out her anger, railing at William John about the unfairness of the Almighty's workings in the Chidester family. He listened to her accusations, then took her into his arms and held her close. When she had quieted, he suggested to her that the tragedies of the winter were not necessarily of the Almighty's doings. He urged her into bed, tucked the coverlet around her, and patted the area over her swollen abdomen. "You must not trouble yourself so. You must think of the new baby on the way." Then, after snuffing out the lamp, he went to his chair by the window and knelt down. When she awoke in the night, the bed was empty beside her and through the darkness she could make out the shadowy form of her husband still kneeling in prayer.

In time William John's gentle reminders that God Almighty was not to blame for fevers and runaway wagons had taken away MaryAnn's bitterness. But it hadn't taken away the great ache she felt every time she looked at Russell.

As for Russell, he had quickly learned to do with one arm what he had always done with two. But learning to live without his sibling playmates was almost more than he could manage. He followed MaryAnn's lumbering figure from room to room, never saying a word. If he wasn't at her side, he could always be found in the room he had shared with his little brothers. Once MaryAnn came upon him there, sitting on the edge of the bed, with a miniature iron wagon in his good hand. It was a favorite toy of all the boys, but Russell wasn't playing with it. He rolled it quietly up and down his useless arm, staring into nothingness all the while. MaryAnn caught her breath and backed away before he saw her. She went directly to her bedroom and, following her husband's example, knelt by William John's chair and cried out to Almighty God. "I can't bear to look at his sufferin', and I'm never goin' to make it through this trial by myself," she sobbed. Not knowing what else to say or to ask, she sat for a while until she felt her body growing stiff and she feared for a moment that she might not be able to pull her pregnant frame up again.

A week later MaryAnn felt the first pangs of birth. The March winds blew about the house as Catarina, MaryAnn's mother, stoked up the fire and put water on to boil. From the bedroom window, MaryAnn could see it was a murky day outside, and wondered where they might send Russell who was much too small to be about during a birthing. Her question was soon answered when Russell appeared at her door asking if he might go with Uncle George to the barn for the day, for George had work to do there. Relieved that George had anticipated their need, she readily gave her consent.

William John, having learned something about delivering babies from his doctor father, assisted Catarina with Mary-Ann. The labor was short, and before two hours had passed William John announced, "We have a seventh son, Mary-Ann." They embraced warmly while Catarina prepared the infant.

They named him Lee William and MaryAnn's heart felt lighter than it had in months. Her joy deepened day by day—not only because of her own delight in her new son, but because Russell took to the baby immediately.

In a short while, young Russell took possession of his new brother. Lee William wasn't even talking yet when Russell first began telling his secrets to his baby brother.

———

For all their lives, even now after Lee William was married, Russell had made his brother privy to all his thoughts. MaryAnn knew that when Russell stomped out of the kitchen, he would go to only one place. "Let him be," she said when William John moved as if to follow him. "He'll go straight to Lee William's. Let him be."

CHAPTER THREE

Generations of Dreamers

William John bided his time for a week. He went to Lee William and Lucy's place and talked over his plans with them. But he said nothing more about Missouri to Russell, who had remained quiet in his anger. At mealtime, Russell ate in silence while George, William John, and Mary-Ann discussed the latest signs of spring. He answered politely enough when spoken to, but made no comments on his own. Each time, when he had eaten, he quickly disappeared, saying that he had some pressing chore to attend to.

From the start, Lee William and Lucy took to the idea like a newborn calf takes to its mother's milk. They eagerly joined William John in his plans and expressed no concern whatsoever over raising their children in a primitive area. Their excitement didn't surprise MaryAnn. She knew her seventh son once had considered following his three older brothers to Tipton. Leaving Indiana would not trouble him. He stayed in Indiana only because his love for farming was stronger than his craving for adventure. Now, thanks to William John, he could have both.

MaryAnn never dreamed that Russell would agree to move to Missouri—until she heard the rest of her husband's plan. Once William John laid it all out, MaryAnn was not surprised that Russell eagerly agreed to go along with his father's ideas.

She carried the breakfast dishes to the dishpan on the stove as she recalled the events of the evening before. The men had been gone a half hour already—time enough for her to have finished the dishes. But she couldn't seem to put her mind to what she was doing. She still found it hard to believe that William John had waited an entire week before saying one word about the shipyards near St. Louis needing men in the office. It made her wonder what other secrets he might be keeping from her.

William John had saved that information as a surprise for Russell, when Russell was ready to listen. And last night he was ready. MaryAnn had seen at once when they sat down to supper that Russell had come out of his mood. He smiled at her as he said, "I'm hungry enough to eat a horse tonight, Mama." She breathed a deep, quiet sigh as she recognized that the air between the men had been cleared.

A moment later she caught a glimpse of her husband's face. A smile pulled at the corners of his lips, and MaryAnn knew at once that William John was anxious to tell them something. While she served up the food, he laid out the rest of his plan to Russell.

"I'll be needing you this season if you decide to come with us, but I heard about a job that put me in mind of you," he began. Russell listened politely but continued to give his attention to his plate of food.

"Lucy's pa is cutting timber for the shipyards at Carondolet," William John continued. "One of their men was scouting timber near Dogwood Creek, and he told me they're needing men in their offices who are good at ciphering." He looked at Russell then, a great smile lighting up his face. "I told him I knew just the man for the job. What do you think?"

What did he think indeed? Russell's head flashed up, food immediately forgotten. With his skill for numbers and his everlasting fascination with boats, of course he would go. There was never any question.

William John's words were hardly out of his mouth when a look of pleasure crossed Russell's face. It was the same look he'd worn as a child plying his grandfather with questions about the big boat that brought him to America. Many times MaryAnn had watched him pull his stool up to her father and beg, "Grandpa, tell me what it was like on the big boat!" And her father would always begin by, "Well, Russell Brean" (he never left out the 'Brean') "I was just about your age . . . " And he would repeat once again such scanty details as he could remember from his Atlantic crossing. Michael Brean, MaryAnn's father, was so young when he made the crossing that he remembered very little. But he did have a drawing of a ship like the one on which the Breans had come to America. He would spread the drawing on his lap and Russell would bend his head closely to see every line as his grandfather explained the various parts of the ship.

Russell had showed the same eagerness last night as he pressed his father for more details. But MaryAnn had hardly listened to the rest of their conversation, for it suddenly came to her that it was settled. They would move to Missouri and leave her family home and her brother George behind. She could see the excitement in her menfolk—an excitement that she wanted to share, but could not find in her heavy heart.

Coming out of her musing, she drew a deep breath and returned to her dishwashing. She wiped the last of the dishes and placed them in a stack on the table. After wringing out the dishcloth she hung it on a rack and grabbed the stove rag. She dampened it in the dish water and dipped it in a box of ashes nearby. She scoured all but the hottest part of the stovetop before rinsing the blackened rag and rehanging it. Woodenly, she walked to the back door, dishpan in hand, and flung the soot-colored water onto the ground. As the cool morning air met her face, MaryAnn decided that the bed-making would have to wait. Right now there was only one place she wanted to be.

———

Whenever MaryAnn needed time to think, she would grab her spade and hoe and head for the Brean family burying grounds west of the house beyond the gooseberry hedge. And this morning she certainly did need to think. As she hurried along the path, she could hear the men working the potato patch just as they had done every April for as far back as she could remember. She breathed deeply of the smell of newly split wood as she passed the neatly stacked supply. Like the sound of the manure wagon in the potato patch, the wood reminded her of all the seasons past. Her father had always insisted that the year's supply be split and stacked in March. He would wave the almanac for emphasis as he quoted its admonition, "Each season has its own work."

MaryAnn's heart caught at the sight of her garden plot. "Unless William John comes to his senses, I've raised my last garden here," she murmured wistfully.

The dew still clung to the bushes when she walked through the hedge and past the tiny graves that held infants from three generations. Her only sister, her two sons, Lee William's twins—she passed them all and walked straight to her father's grave.

The earth on Michael Leland Brean's bury hole had a fresh-turned look, for he had lain there less than a year. MaryAnn still felt empty inside at the sight of the grave. She jabbed her hoe at a clump of weeds, jerked them out, and threw them aside. She attacked the next clump and the next, until the grave was clean. "Who do you s'pose will keep off the weeds if I go clean to Missouri?" she asked out loud. Then, leaning on her hoe, she burst into tears.

MaryAnn hated tears, but this morning she couldn't help herself. Her thoughts were so jumbled, and who could she talk to? *It was a mistake to come here*, she scolded herself, as she snuffed her nose several times. She reasoned that even if a body could speak from the grave, there would be no understanding for her in this place.

"I don't reckon I'd get a bit of sympathy from any of you," she reproached the silent graves. "Truth to tell, you'd all be right there pitchin' for William John with his big plans. You'd all disown me for gettin' so worked up about removin' to the frontier." She grabbed the corner of her apron and dabbed furiously at her eyes before moving to a patch of weeds between the graves.

There were only three full-size graves in the burial ground, and the people who lay in them had all been dreamers. Great-grandfather Ian Brean had followed his dream across the Atlantic. And Catarina Schmidt Brean, MaryAnn's mother, had not only crossed the Atlantic, but had also crossed the country alone, driving a wagon to the Indiana frontier. As for MaryAnn's father, he had been orphaned by Indians two years after he came to America and had been

raised by his grandfather, Ian. There was no denying it—
these people had known real hardship and would feel little
sympathy for a grown woman who feared it so.

Bending over her work, MaryAnn felt her eyes filling with
tears once more. She shoved her spade deep into the ground
and attacked an uncommonly long root. Angrily she yanked
it out. "This is exactly what William John's doin' to me. He's
yankin' me up like a bunch of weeds from the earth. Why
couldn't he have his dream without jerkin' me out of my
home?"

It was the only home she had ever known—a home where
four generations of her family had lived. Now William John
was asking her to leave it.

The house was built by Ian Brean, and while MaryAnn
had never known her great-grandfather, she knew his story
well, for her father often told it.

Michael Brean had been only seven years old when he
came with his parents and grandfather to America. Ian's
other son, Great-uncle Patrick, stayed behind in Ireland. In
America, the Breans had staked out a farm in Tennessee,
where for two years they hunted and farmed and schemed
how they might send for Patrick and his young wife and
babies.

The year Michael was nine, he and his grandfather came
home from hunting and found the cabin in smoking ruins. It
was Michael who came upon the bodies, each pierced through
with an Indian spear. That night he woke up screaming from
the memory, and his "Indian dreams" did not cease until long
after he was grown.

Nothing survived the fire except Ian's fiddle and the painting of his wife who lay buried in County Cork, Ireland. The
horses they had ridden for the hunt were all Ian had to show

for his work in America. The next day the old man and young Michael set out for Indiana with nothing but the clothes on their backs, Ian's fiddle, and the painting of Ian's wife.

Together the grandfather and grandson carved out another farm near White River. The house that Ian built was much too large for the two of them, but Ian Brean never gave up his dream of bringing the rest of his family from Ireland. Building a great house to accommodate them had been his way of keeping his dream alive.

But there were problems on both sides of the Atlantic— potato famines, wars, sickness—and by and by Ian Brean died without ever having brought even one more Brean from County Cork.

MaryAnn moved on to Ian's grave and shook her head as she glanced at the simple marker that read, *Ian Brean, the first Brean to come to America.* According to her father, it had been Ian's last wish to have the grave so marked. It was his way of reminding his grandson to carry on with the plans they had made for the Brean family.

And MaryAnn's father had tried. Even after Uncle Patrick and his two sons died in County Cork, Michael had tried to help the one remaining grandson and his family to emigrate from Ireland. How many times had MaryAnn heard her father announce his latest plan for bringing the Irish kin to America? How many times had she seen her mother greet the announcement with a flurry of preparations as if the emigrants were arriving on the next stage? But her father, like his grandfather before him, died without ever bringing anyone from County Cork to live in the great log house.

Instead, the house had been filled with Michael and Catarina's family, and by and by with MaryAnn's boys. Each time MaryAnn gave birth Catarina greeted the event with

"Gott be praised, daughter! It's gut zat you haf boys. Vat vudt you do vif girls?" And she was right. MaryAnn who had always shunned housework, preferring instead to work outdoors with her brothers, would nod in agreement. Then she and Catarina would hug each other and laugh and cry a little.

Catarina had been the only female companion MaryAnn had ever had or wanted and she still missed her. Coming to her mother's grave, MaryAnn pulled a few weeds that had grown there. She grew suddenly conscious of the struggles of the German immigrant woman who had endured great hardships in order to pursue a dream.

Catarina Schmidt had left her homeland with a husband and two young children. They left behind them a third child—buried in a tiny grave near the village church. On the worst Atlantic crossing of the year, Catarina gave birth to her fourth child. A week after they arrived in New York, both her husband and the baby died of ship's fever.

Two years later, Catarina loaded her two sons and her few goods onto a wagon and set out for the Indiana frontier. Ian Brean had been in his grave nearly a decade when the widow Schmidt stopped her wagon at the log house and handed the bachelor, Michael Brean, a letter from the land office in the village. The letter explained that this widow who spoke no English had just purchased the adjoining farm. Would Michael be good enough to show her the way?

The way MaryAnn's father told the tale, he had known from that first meeting that Catarina Schmidt was the woman he wanted to marry. After encountering the German woman who had come so far to give her children a piece of the frontier, Michael knew he could never admire another woman as he admired Catarina.

When Catarina married Michael, she came to the great house with two young sons who quickly learned to call Michael "Papa," but never took his name. Catarina bore three children to Michael, but the first died in infancy. They raised four children—her two boys, and George and Mary-Ann—all in the same log house.

MaryAnn had heard the story of her parents' first meeting a hundred times or more and never tired of it, but this morning the recalling of it made her uncomfortable. She could almost feel her parents accusing her. They had never balked at hardships.

She spread her dew-dampened skirt to catch the drying rays of the sun and peered back at her home. She could see the second floor corner bedroom. It was the room William John had slept in the summer he came to board at the Brean home. There her seven boys had been born, and there two of them had died. This time the flood of memories brought anger instead of tears. "I don't want to leave my home, William John," she muttered defiantly. "But I don't get a choice, do I?"

She glanced at the graves once more, acknowledging that if bones could talk, they would answer her, "No, MaryAnn, you don't get a choice."

Straightening her somewhat thin frame, MaryAnn collected her tools and walked down the slope toward the house.

She deposited the tools at the kitchen door, brushed the dirt from her skirt, pushed back her hair, and went in. She dipped some water into the washpan and splashed her face. "No need for the menfolk to know I spent the morning cryin' my eyes out," she murmured. "Likely they'll all be here for dinner today." She looked at her face in a small mirror near the washpan, as if searching for some inherited remnant of the courage of her parents and grandparents. She didn't take note that her black hair was still lovely, even with a few strands of grey, at the age of forty-six, and she couldn't know that her blue-black eyes—despite her earlier tears— reflected a calmness and strength that her family depended on. She shook her head sadly, for the MaryAnn she saw was homesick already.

Heirlooms

~~~

MaryAnn stirred up the fire in the cookstove. She would need the oven for baking cornbread. It was more than an hour before the men came in. By then, all traces of her morning's grief had vanished.

"George has gone to the village, MaryAnn," announced William John, wiping his hands on the towel by the washpan. "He won't be here for dinner, but Lee William's come." He smiled at her and seemed not to notice that she could not smile in return.

Lee William greeted her and smiled. "We're making plans, Mama."

Of course, she thought. *Of course you are, Son.* She looked at twenty-year-old Lee William's lean, six-foot-four frame and saw her own husband reflected there. Both were tall and lanky. Both had deep brown eyes that seemed to see everything, and they had the same brown hair. But Lee William's hair, unlike his father's, was slightly curly. *Such a handsome young man*, MaryAnn observed silently. *No wonder Lucy was attracted to him.*

Russell said nothing, but even he was smiling. The three sat down. MaryAnn served up fried bacon, beans, and cornbread. Then she drew up her own chair and listened quietly as the men talked.

"Pa," Russell began, after eating a full helping of beans, "I've been wondering about something. How'd you ever convince Lee William to go to Missouri? He's too much of an abolitionist to move to a slave state!" MaryAnn squirmed uncomfortably, anticipating the usual argument between the three men over the slavery issue. Russell seldom raised the subject, but he was always quick to challenge what the other men said.

Without giving his father a chance to speak, Lee William broke in. "I can answer that for myself," he said, speaking more sharply than usual. "There's not that much difference in the two states, Russell. I can't see as Indiana thinks any more of the Negroes than any of the slave states do. They won't allow them to live here, free or bound. I reckon one state's as good as another these days. Likely, nothing will get better until the abolitionists get a hearing."

"Don't be taken in, Lee William," Russell cautioned. "Abolitionists are going to cause a blood bath in this country yet."

"Listen to you! You read everything William Lloyd Garrison writes."

"I don't happen to agree with everything I read. And I don't figure Garrison to be a radical," Russell countered.

"Maybe he should be. Most likely, he won't be solving the problem with ink."

William John looked from one son to the other before breaking into the conversation. "I should tell you both that things are stirring a bit in Missouri right now—not on

28

Dogwood Creek, mind you, but some of the families there have kinfolk up along the Missouri River, and they say there's a heap of unrest there right now. Could be trouble."

MaryAnn usually kept quiet when her husband and sons argued politics, but she could hold her peace no longer at this last revelation about Missouri. "William John, if there's goin' to be bloodshed, I don't think we should be takin' Lucy and little Arial into such a place."

The men grew suddenly silent and looked at MaryAnn. Then Russell and Lee William glanced at their father and waited.

"First off, nobody's *taking* anybody anywhere," William John said gently. He crumbled cornbread into his milk before continuing. "Second, the trouble is apt to be in Kansas, if it comes. And that's a ways from Dogwood Creek. The way I figure it, if a real war comes, Indiana won't be near as safe as Dogwood Creek."

"What makes you say that, Pa?" Russell prodded. For once MaryAnn felt glad that Russell habitually challenged any opinion his father expressed. She leaned forward, eager to hear William John's explanation.

"Dogwood Creek is way off the main road—maybe a dozen homes scattered along the banks. Most people are two, three miles from their nearest neighbor. It's not likely that a lot of people even know about the place."

"There's not even a settlement?" Russell dropped his fork against the edge of his plate.

"Can't say as there is. But we'll get mail at Carrick's Mill. An old man and his boys operate a grist mill near the county line, and the road ends there right now. The mail drops there three times a week."

29

Russell looked his brother straight on and said, "Lee William, sounds like my little niece will grow up just like her mama—not a day of schooling in her life."

Lee William's face flushed, but he answered the taunt evenly. "You know Pa will teach a school there. Anyway, it'll be a few years before Arial's ready."

MaryAnn saw William John's face grow sober for a moment as if he were remembering their own school ruckus just over a month ago. She could see he hadn't really forgiven himself for losing that fight. *No wonder he's bent on runnin' off to Missouri,* she mused.

"I s'pose your little Tennessee bride will feel right at home there, little brother, if it's as primitive as it sounds," Russell persisted. He often referred to Lucy in this manner, especially when he was in a disagreeable mood.

Lee William did not answer, but he gave Russell a hard stare. MaryAnn and William John sat silently by. This was the one subject her sons could not discuss. At first MaryAnn had thought Russell was resentful because he had met the beautiful and slender Lucy first, had in fact called on her at Jubal Tate's cabin. But gradually MaryAnn realized that Russell didn't resent Lee William's marrying Lucy.

What he purely does resent is that Lee William doesn't have as much time for him now that he has a wife and child, MaryAnn thought. It didn't seem to matter that he and Lee William were still privy to each other's deepest thoughts. It wasn't enough anymore. Russell couldn't seem to help himself. At times he simply had to spill out his resentment of the "little Tennessee bride," as he was wont to call his brother's wife.

Russell sat silent under Lee William's gaze. At length he rubbed his lame arm slightly and stammered, "I got no call to criticize Lucy, Lee William. I know she's been a right good wife to you. I'm sorry." He shifted uncomfortably in his chair.

Lee William, who could never stay angry with his brother, smiled then, and Russell changed the subject. Turning to his father, he asked cautiously, "How long do you expect me to stay at Dogwood Creek?"

William John ate the last spoonful of cornbread from his glass. After draining the last of the milk, he smiled at Russell and spoke politely as if choosing his words carefully. "I'd be obliged if you'd help us with settling and all. I reckon before winter you could be working for the boatyards—if you're interested. They need people like you. The way I figure it, you'd be right for that job and it would be plumb right for you. But you might want to think on it awhile. You might want to change your mind."

But of course Russell didn't want to change his mind. He had no need to think longer about it. The three ate their dinner, paying no mind to MaryAnn's sober mood. When they got up to leave, William John suggested that she should begin to make preparations and added that they were off to do the same.

————————

A week later, MaryAnn sat in a corner of the parlor, packing quilts into a chest. A frown creased her brow. Somehow it didn't seem right. How could a man and woman be married long enough to raise a family and still be able to fit everything they owned into one trunk?

Suddenly she caught a glimmer of what William John meant when he said the Brean family home wasn't his. *Most folks who take it into their heads to move to a place as far away as Missouri have a sale. But William John and me—we don't have anything to sell! I reckon George owns nearly everything in this house,* she thought.

But, being quite honest with herself, MaryAnn admitted that there were things bothering her that were more important than not owning enough plunder to hold a decent sale. Ever since William John had come back with his horse, he was like a different man. It wasn't just that he was excited over homesteading a place of his own on Dogwood Creek. There was something else about him that worried her. He seemed secretive somehow, as if he hadn't yet told her all there was to tell. When he described the spot he had picked for their homestead, she pressed him for details, asking how he had come upon that particular place. He ignored her question and changed the subject. At first, she thought he hadn't heard her. But when it happened again, she felt a panic. What could cause William John to act so peculiar? She had begun to feel as if she didn't really know her husband anymore.

She folded the last quilt and plopped it in the chest. "There. That leaves just the right space for Great-grandmother Brean's picture. At least that belongs to me," she whispered to herself.

The painting, which measured twelve inches high and eighteen inches wide, hung above the mantel. It was mounted in the same wooden frame that had held it for almost forty years. How often MaryAnn had stood and stared at the painting when she was growing up! How many times she had imagined romantic tales about that young woman perched on a jaunting cart in faraway Ireland. More than once MaryAnn had been told that she resembled the woman in the picture. Once when her parents were standing near the painting, Catarina had said to Michael in her broken English, "MaryAnn ist ze same as ze picture. She looks like ze grossmutter, ja?" MaryAnn's father had shrugged and admitted that he couldn't remember his grandmother, but he agreed that their daughter did resemble the woman in the painting.

On MaryAnn's wedding day, her father had given her the painting. She remembered him standing in front of the mantel. Without taking the painting down, Michael Brean had declared, "From now on, MaryAnn, this picture belongs to you." He had been embarrassed over her expression of delight and had carefully freed himself from her unusually impulsive hug. And then, as if not knowing what else to say, he had told her about another painting, one that had been left behind in County Cork.

"In Ireland there's another painting just like this one, except in that one, my grandfather Ian is sitting in the cart. He used to talk about it sometimes. A friend painted both pictures for them when my grandparents got married."

Eagerly MaryAnn had pressed him for more details. "But why would your grandfather Ian leave one painting in Ireland?"

"It was his link with Patrick and the others who stayed behind," her father had said simply. "Of course, he planned for them to follow him to America and to bring the painting with them. But, well, you know that never happened."

She had never heard her father speak of the other painting again, but afterwards MaryAnn had often seen him standing before the fireplace, staring at the painting of her great-grandmother. Sometimes he stood there every night for a week. And then, he would stop staring and announce his latest plan to bring the Irish kin to America. Then MaryAnn would imagine that soon there would be two pictures hanging above the mantel.

She sighed heavily. *Well, it never happened. And now I'm takin' the one that has hung there since this house was built.* Somehow, she felt as if she were destroying the tie between the two sides of the family just by taking the picture with her to some faraway place. Once she took it away, there would be nothing left to link the house that Ian Brean built to the family left in Ireland.

MaryAnn ran her fingers over the top quilt, tracing the intricate log cabin pattern. Catarina had made the quilt the first year that she lived in the great log house. It was her way of thanking Michael for the home he had provided for her and her sons. The quilt had kept her and Michael warm through all the winters of their marriage. After she died, Michael folded the quilt away and never slept under it again. MaryAnn shook her head as she realized that every event in the Brean family—births, deaths, marriages—all were tied to that log house. The house, with all its history, was her link with the family. And now she would be cutting that link. She was so engrossed in her thoughts that she did not hear her brother come in.

"MaryAnn . . ."

MaryAnn jumped. "George! You shouldn't sneak up on a body. You startled me."

"I didn't sneak, MaryAnn. You were thinkin' on something mighty deep. And from the looks of that frown, I'd say it was none too pleasant." He looked uncharacteristically sober himself, standing there with his arms crossed. Just two years older than MaryAnn, he had the Brean look—stockily built, black hair, dark eyes. There had been little about either of them that marked them as Catarina's children.

"You always knew me better than anyone, didn't you, George?" She felt wistful, anticipating how she would miss her brother.

"You followed me around from the time you could walk, so I guess I oughta know you." George chuckled. "Right now I'll wager you're none too happy about movin' to Missouri."

"It's not Missouri—exactly." MaryAnn glanced away and chewed on her lip.

"Then what?" George prodded. He leaned against the doorframe and waited for her to explain.

"George, I've lived here all my life, and until two weeks ago I never even thought about the fact that it's someone else's home—first our parents', then yours. William John and me don't even own enough to make a sale!" It wasn't easy for MaryAnn to put her thoughts into words, even with her brother.

"Oh, MaryAnn, you know it's as much your home as mine. I wouldn't ever put you out. I don't even want you to go. Let me talk to William John."

"It's too late for that, George. William John has set his mind to go to Missouri. And it has nothin' to do with you or with livin' in your home. It has to do with William John havin' to find a new dream." She paused and pushed back a stray lock of hair before she explained. "When the White Creek school closed last month, it was as if he lost his whole reason to live. He fought for free schools for so long and when he lost again, he couldn't find it in himself to keep on fightin' that

35

battle. He's got nothin' left except farmin' someone else's farm and that's not enough for William John anymore. The idea of homesteadin' on Dogwood Creek has given him somethin' to plan for again."

"What about you, MaryAnn? What about what *you* want?" George crossed to where she sat, took her by the shoulders, and searched her blue-black eyes.

"I reckon I can see the difference in William John since he come back from Missouri. And I like what I see, only . . ."

"Only what?"

"William John's actin' mighty strange. It's like nothin' else in life matters to him anymore except homesteadin' in Missouri. I'm scared, George. It scares me to see him like that." She shook her head at the thought. "Then there's so many questions, and he don't seem to have time to answer 'em. You know, I still don't know how come he picked Dogwood Creek. Just this morning I asked him, but he went off to the village in a big hurry sayin' that he was buyin' a new steel blade plow and some seed and that I should be ready to leave within the week. He never answered my question." MaryAnn reached over and smoothed the top quilt in the chest once more, even though it was perfectly packed.

"I thought Dogwood Creek was where he found his horse."

"Oh, that's true enough. But that's what bothers me most. Whenever anyone asks about that fool horse he looks away or chews on his lip. I know William John. There's somethin' botherin' that man, and I would be easier about movin' if I knew what it was." MaryAnn's voice rose in emphasis as she made this declaration.

"Maybe not, MaryAnn. Maybe William John figures there's some things you're better off not knowin'."

"I don't like it. He's never kept secrets before." Having said it, MaryAnn realized what was bothering her most about the move. It wasn't just that she was being forced to remove to some strange place and start a new home; it was the change in William John, the husband she had been married to for thirty years. She felt like she didn't know him anymore—like he had shut her out of everything that was going on inside. If she were no longer privy to his dreams and plans, how could she help but feel shut out of his heart?

George patted her shoulder tenderly. "Whatever it is, MaryAnn, he'll tell you when the time comes. William John's a good man—you've always been able to trust him. You sure you don't want me to try to get him to stay?"

"No, George. Wouldn't do any good. He's bound to go, and nothin's goin' to stand in his way."

MaryAnn rose from her stool and smoothed her apron. She crossed the room to stand before the painting of Great-grandmother Brean. She touched the picture lightly with her finger, tracing the green hills that towered above the lakes of Killarney. She gazed into the face of the young woman seated on the jaunting cart.

Aloud she said, "I can't imagine Great-grandmother's picture hangin' anywhere but right here in this room, but I can't bear to go to Missouri without it either."

George crossed the room and stood beside her. "It's yours to take, MaryAnn," he said softly. "Papa gave it to you on your weddin' day." He reached his arm across her shoulder and hugged her briefly.

MaryAnn nodded. "I know Papa gave it to me, but then William John moved in with the family and the picture kept hanging where it hung from the time this house was built.

It don't seem right somehow to take it down. Room won't look right without it."

"Never mind about the room, MaryAnn. Great-grandma Brean's picture will be a little bit of home to take with you. Besides, maybe I'll have another paintin' to put in its place before too long." George's eyes twinkled as MaryAnn abruptly turned toward him.

Her own eyes widened in disbelief. "What! Whatever can you mean, George? Sounds as if William John's not the only one with secrets."

"There's no secret, Sister. But I did write to Sean Brean in County Cork and I asked him to come to America. You know how Papa and his grandpa before him wanted to bring the rest of the family over. The last we heard, Sean and his brother, Casey, were the only two left."

"Great-grandsons of Patrick Brean."

"That's right. I figured to help them get started, if they'll come."

"Oh, George, how wonderful! Do you plan for them to live with you here? Will they help you farm?"

"Whoa, MaryAnn! Slow down." George laughed lightly. "I haven't made any plans for them. They'll have to decide that for themselves after they come." He scratched his chin thoughtfully as he added, "That is, *if* they come."

MaryAnn glanced at the painting once again. "Do you s'pose they'll bring the other paintin'?" she asked.

"Well, that was the plan. You remember the story. When the last Brean left Ireland, he was to bring the matchin' picture. So you see that old wall might not be vacant for long."

As he spoke, George took down the painting and handed it to MaryAnn. "Here," he said, "put this in your trunk. When you look at it in your new home, think of me and all our Irish immigrant kin here in Indiana."

Clasping the painting against her breast, MaryAnn smiled at her brother for the first time that afternoon. "Think of it, George," she said, "maybe you will make Papa's dream come true."

George shook his head slightly. "I'm not writin' to Irish kin for Papa, MaryAnn. It's my own dream now. It's somethin' *I* want to do. There's somethin' we all have to remember about dreams—tryin' to make someone else's dream come true can be mighty burdensome." Again he caught her by the shoulder and pierced her eyes with his own. "Don't ever forget that, MaryAnn."

Before MaryAnn had time to ponder her brother's words, the kitchen door flew open, and William John walked in.

"It's done!" he called out happily. "Everything is ready, MaryAnn. Can you be ready by first light tomorrow?"

She went to the trunk, placed the painting inside, and snapped the lid shut. Then, returning her husband's smile she said, "That takes care of everything, William John. I reckon I'm ready right now." She spoke with more confidence than she felt, and she hoped that her voice did not betray the ache she already felt for the home she was leaving behind.

CHAPTER FIVE

Dogwood Creek

———— ∽ ————

Their leaving was delayed two days, for George needed the team a while longer. He had insisted that William John take the team, declaring that in spite of their advanced age, they were still the strongest work horses in the county and were well suited for pulling the wagon to Missouri.

On the last afternoon, George also gave up Ian Brean's fiddle.

Lucy had come by the great house on her way home from the graveyard. "It was hard seein' our babies' bury holes for the last time," she said to MaryAnn, her cornflower blue eyes glinting with a hint of earlier tears. MaryAnn hugged her daughter-in-law clumsily. She wanted to comfort Lucy somehow, but she couldn't find the words—she never could at such times. William John was so much better with words. And Catarina had always known just what to say. But MaryAnn wasn't like her husband or her mother. Like her father Michael, MaryAnn always felt as though her tongue were tied down.

As she stood wondering what to say to Lucy, George came into the room, fiddle in hand. He handed it to Lucy, reminding her that the fiddle had gone everywhere the painting of Ian Brean's wife had gone. "I reckon it'd be bad luck to change that," he said. "Anyway, Lee William's the real fiddler in the family. I want him to have it."

They left at dawn the next morning. George hitched the team himself, while it was still dark, and drove the wagon from the barnlot to the house gate. While the men loaded everything by lantern light, MaryAnn and Lucy fixed breakfast. Two-year-old Arial slept peacefully in the downstairs bedroom where Lee William and Lucy had spent the night. MaryAnn fought back tears as she took the pan of biscuits from the oven and called the men for one last meal together. They ate hurriedly, making nervous little jokes back and forth, and MaryAnn sensed that the men both dreaded and anticipated the final moment of leave-taking. When they had finished, they hurried to their preparations, leaving the women to clean the table.

It was done quickly and Lucy went to check on Arial. MaryAnn walked to the front door, stepped outside, and looked at the shadowy scene before her. The first streaks of daylight revealed the familiar lines of the house. The squared logs, perfectly dovetailed at the corners of the house, appeared sturdier than she had noticed before. The plum orchard, in full bloom, stretched along the south side of the house just beyond the road that ran through the Brean farm. She breathed deeply of the cool morning air and hurried to the wagon, knowing it must be time to leave. She found George standing apart, silently watching, and walked to his side.

Lee William handed Lucy into the wagon, and they settled the sleeping Arial beside her. Then he joined Russell, and they mounted the saddle horses.

Reluctant to tell her brother good-bye, MaryAnn stood beside him until William John was already on the wagon seat with the lines poised and ready. She gazed up the hill towards her garden, imagining the peas and lettuce that always grew there. She wished that she could walk the fields one more time and smell the new-plowed ground. At last, she embraced George and allowed him to help her to her place beside William John.

"We're obliged to you, George—for everythin'," she said. For a moment their eyes held, and she could feel his encouragement, but they said no more.

George turned and patted the flank of the mare he had raised from a filly. William John snapped the lines and clucked, "Giddyap."

As the wagon rolled away, MaryAnn waved once, then set her eyes straight ahead and never looked back until they made camp for the night.

———

From the first night, they fell into an easy routine. While MaryAnn and Lucy fixed their meal over the open fire, the men took care of the horses. After a simple supper, Lee William brought out the fiddle and Russell played his French harp.

It was the fiddle that kept MaryAnn from tears as day by day the miles lengthened between her and her home. Her father, who had learned the fiddle from Ian Brean himself, had been a fiddler known in three counties. Lee William had been his pupil. Somehow the nightly fiddling raised MaryAnn's spirits. Listening to the familiar tunes helped her fight the feeling of being rooted up like some weed out of her garden.

During the day she pondered over William John's actions. Cheerful as a robin in spring, he'd whistle constantly, pausing only when he talked about his homesteading plans. Yet once when MaryAnn questioned him about how he came to choose Dogwood Creek, he pretended not to hear and went on whistling. When she pressed, he grew silent. Then looking very sober, he told her, "I'll explain some day, MaryAnn." And he drove the rest of the day in silence.

His mysterious behavior troubled MaryAnn. William John had always been such a talker, telling MaryAnn the smallest details of everything he hoped to do. And when he accomplished something that made him happy, MaryAnn was the first to know. He'd always told her about the difficult student who finally passed to the next reader—or the one who seemed to make no progress at all. William John never bothered to sort out the encouraging news from the discouraging. Whatever was on his mind he'd spill out to MaryAnn. She wondered gloomily if he would ever be like that again.

———

At last, in mid-May, they came to Dogwood Creek. They camped the last night near a spring at the head of the creek. In spite of their weariness from the long journey, the travelers felt little need for sleep. Anticipating all that the next day would bring, they talked excitedly around the campfire, plying William John with questions. Even Mary-Ann entered in, asking her husband what they would see

44

come daylight. Lee William played his fiddle for an hour after the women went to bed. MaryAnn fell asleep to the strains of "Old Aunt Sally, There's a Bug on Me." Dreamily, she remembered how as a child, she had often fallen asleep to this same melody as her father played Ian Brean's fiddle.

The next morning William John was stirring long before first light, but he didn't build a fire, and for the first time on their journey they did without their morning coffee. Just as MaryAnn opened her mouth to complain, William John grabbed her in his arms and danced her around the wagon until she panted for breath. Then, whistling as he went, he scurried away to tend to the horses.

The family satisfied their hunger with such cold leavings from last night's supper as they could find, and MaryAnn was seized with a great wonder about what could excite a forty-eight-year-old man so that he became young again.

When they came to Solomon's Ridge, she knew.

A faint odor of lilacs and wild grape blossoms hung in the air. Little clumps of johnny-jump-ups bloomed here and there, and in every old tree snag MaryAnn could see signs of bluebirds building their nests. On the road, they passed the remains of an ancient cabin, and William John pointed out the pee-wees, building under the eaves, and the little jenny wrens, flitting about the knotholes in a broken-down rail fence. Other than that, he hardly said a word. He just sniffed the air, looked at the sky, and smiled every few minutes at MaryAnn until at last he halted the team under a great oak tree.

William John tied the lines and, scrambling down from the wagon, pointed to the scene below them. "There's where your very own home will be, Mrs. Chidester," he said proudly.

He pointed down the hill to a flat area where a young black walnut tree stood. Beyond it, a dozen yards or more, the land

45

sloped gently down to a narrow creek. "We'll build our cabin this side of the walnut tree," he explained. "You can't see from here, but that creek is fed by a good spring down there in the rocks. We'll dig it out some and make a springhouse if you like. We'll have a ways to carry water to the house, but I'll fix you a place to do your washing down by the spring. You'll have the best cabin around, MaryAnn, you'll see."

But MaryAnn wasn't concerned about what kind of house they would build. She was plotting her garden. She could see exactly where she would put it. She knew already that in this place, as in Indiana, she would find every reason to spend her time outdoors.

She was aware of William John still talking about his plans, but she was no longer listening. Waves of excitement rushed over her as she saw all the possibilities of home on Dogwood Creek. She shook her head. *Maybe I've been in this wagon too long,* she reasoned to herself. *Maybe that's why ever'thin' looks so good. But if the rest of the seasons are half as remarkable as May, I'm goin' to enjoy these hills.* She felt positively heady looking out at the scene below her.

And then it came to her. William John had known, of course. He had known all along that once she saw this piece of land, once she came to Solomon's Ridge, she would under-stand everything—she would understand his excitement over moving to Missouri. He had known she would fall in love with Dogwood Creek.

———

MaryAnn stood beside her husband under the great oak tree, as William John poured out his plans for their new home. Lucy, still in the wagon, stretched her neck to see the scene below. Lee William and Russell reined their horses around for a better view.

"We'll build the barn right here on this hill," he said. "We'll have it up before winter comes—"

"You knew, didn't you?" MaryAnn interrupted.

William John looked at her, a puzzled expression on his face.

She smiled. "You knew once I saw this place—I declare, William John, I can't wait to put in my garden! It has to be right there behind where you aim to build the house. I can already see it—onions, lettuce, squash . . . Of course the gooseberry cutting I brought along will have to go near the garden gate, so we have to decide right away where that's goin' to be."

William John chuckled as MaryAnn talked on. When she stopped for breath, he pointed to a row of sycamore trees down by the creek. "Arial will be ready to climb around on that biggest sycamore before we know it," he said, glancing toward the child and her mother in the wagon. A clump of hazelnut bushes stretched up the hill beyond the sycamores. William John suggested that the chicken house be built there.

MaryAnn nodded in agreement and glanced around the scene once more. The plot where William John intended to build the house was surrounded by trees—walnut, oak, sycamore, butternut, and elm. A gully ran alongside the area, separating it from the hill just north of where they stood. As her eyes fell on that hill, MaryAnn drew in her breath. "That looks like an apple orchard, William John. Has somebody lived here before?"

"No, not so far as anyone can remember. People around here seem to think Johnny Appleseed came through these parts. The orchard's been there for as long as anyone can remember." He looked up at Lee William, still seated on his saddle horse. "There's a nice piece of land on the other side of the orchard, Son. Maybe one of these days we can put up a second cabin for you and Lucy."

Lee William smiled down at Lucy who patted her growing stomach and said, "I reckon we'll need it in another year or two."

"It sounds wonderful—your own cabin near an apple orchard," MaryAnn said enthusiastically to her daughter-in-law. "But no need to hurry. We'll all manage in the big cabin William John aims to build below this oak—"

She stopped, remembering about William John's horse. "So this is where you found your horse?"

The look on his face told her that she shouldn't ask anything more. A moment ago she had thought he would never stop talking. But now he stood as silent as the oak tree at which he stared. The boys both looked at her and then at William John. Lee William twisted uneasily in his saddle, and Russell tugged at his withered arm.

Well, I reckon they know somethin' I don't know, she said to herself. She waited for her husband to speak. But when he did, it was as if he hadn't heard her question.

"We'd best be heading on," he said, climbing back on the wagon. "Lucy must be anxious to see her pa, and I want to get to the Bennett place as soon as we can. Mr. Bennett said he'd find us a temporary place to stay. He even asked if we'd like to move in with them until our cabin's built."

MaryAnn, already cross because she was sure her husband was hiding something from her, spoke sharply. "I don't want to move in with strangers, William John. I'll not be beholden to people I don't even know. I'd as soon camp in this wagon 'til the house is built."

"Oh MaryAnn, you'd soon get tired of that. It will be awhile yet. We've got to get some crops in first. We're getting a late start as it is."

MaryAnn didn't answer him. The excitement she had felt a moment ago dimmed in the shadow of William John's secretiveness. The prospects of a new garden could hardly make up for the dissatisfaction she felt with her distant and moody husband. She set her jaw resolutely and stared at the countryside until they came to Jubal Tate's new timber operation.

The sun was almost in its midday spot when William John drove the team off the main road and followed a newly cut wagon trace. Silently, MaryAnn took note of the forest in which they found themselves. Patches of sunlight pierced through the timber. *Once the trees are fully leafed out, it'll be dark as the inside of a cow's belly in here,* MaryAnn thought. The dense woods deepened her uncomfortable feeling that she had suddenly become a woman of the frontier.

Over the rumble of the wagon wheels MaryAnn heard the measured rhythm of a woodsman's ax. She speculated that this must be Jubal Tate's place but stubbornly refused to ask William John.

There was no need, for he called over his shoulder to Lucy. "I reckon that's your pa at the end of that axe handle. This is where he's cutting timber." As he spoke they came into a small clearing where Jubal stood hewing a fallen tree. The sight of a familiar face might have lifted MaryAnn's spirits under different circumstances. But Jubal Tate looked for all the world like a pioneer himself, reminding her again that they had come to a sparsely settled area. His scraggly hair fell to his shoulders from beneath a broadbrimmed hat that was jammed tightly on his head. His long-flowing beard bore the unmistakable stains of tobacco. His jaw puffed out over the quid he was never without. Dressed in a homespun shirt and suspendered trousers, he looked up as William John pulled the team to a halt.

"Hey there, Jubal," William John called, as he tied the reins. "I brought you company!"

"Theeeey!" Jubal exclaimed, spitting a stream of tobacco on the ground. He struck his axe into a stump and hurried toward the wagon. Somewhat stiffly, Lucy climbed down from the rear of the wagon and fell into her father's arms. She kissed him on the cheek. He swung Arial up into one arm and with his free hand shook hands with the others.

Behind the trees, its stove pipe barely visible, stood Jubal's hastily built cabin. With Jubal and Arial leading the way, they all piled into the tiny one-room structure. A bed protruded from one wall, and in one corner stood a rough table and three stools hewn from logs. A small cookstove was the only other furnishing.

"It ain't much, Lee William," Jubal said. "But you and Lucy are welcome to stay the season. It'd be mighty good to have you and Arial around. 'Course there's a big cabin goin' to be empty right soon. Smith family movin' on, 'cordin' to Logan Bennett." Turning to William John, he continued, "Bennett sent word that I should tell you 'bout it, also said that iffen you wuz to git here afore the Smiths left that you'd be right welcome to stay with them."

William John turned to MaryAnn. She saw the question in his eyes, as if he hoped that she would agree to the plan before he even asked. She resolved not to make it easy for him. *Let him ask outright,* she thought. *Then . . . well, then we'll see.* Her jaw tightened under her husband's gaze. William John waited briefly, then said to Jubal, "I reckon we'll make out with the wagon until the Smith cabin's ready. MaryAnn doesn't take much to moving in with strangers."

"Pshaw, ma'am, ain't no strangers on Dogwood Creek," Jubal exclaimed. He waved his hands and laughed as he spoke. Then, clearing his throat first, he added, "Ma'am, I'd be proud to have you'uns stay with me. Might be crowded, but don't reckon it'd be fer long. Way Logan tells it, the Smiths are pret' nigh ready to go."

MaryAnn glanced around the tiny cabin. Jubal Tate, like the birds who came and went with the seasons, seldom stayed in one place for long. His cabin had all the markings of a timber man's temporary dwelling. The unhewn, bark-covered log walls had no chinking. Here and there, tiny shafts of sunlight shone between the cracks. Half-hewn logs formed a puncheon floor, giving off a pleasant odor of unseasoned timber. There was room on the floor for one, maybe two, pallets, but no more. "Thank you kindly, Jubal," she said, "but we couldn't . . . "

In the end it was Lucy and Jubal together who solved the problem. Lucy and MaryAnn would sleep in Jubal's bed, and Jubal would sleep on a pallet on the floor with Arial beside him on her own little pallet. The other men would sleep under the wagon.

CHAPTER SIX

William John's Secret

───────────── ∞ ─────────────

O n their fourth morning on Dogwood Creek—after MaryAnn had been cramped up in Jubal's cabin for three long days—William John suggested that they pay a visit to the Bennetts. Eagerly MaryAnn agreed. She put on a clean apron and combed her hair while William John hitched the team to the wagon. They rode along the ridge for almost an hour, coming at last to the Bennetts' frame house. William John explained to MaryAnn that Logan and Cora would be their nearest neighbors, once their cabin was built.

The two-story white house sat on the rise of a hill. One porch wrapped across the front and around the east side of the house. A second-story porch extended across the upper front. On its banister hung several quilts. Beyond, MaryAnn could see curtains flapping through open windows. The door to the upstairs porch stood open. MaryAnn took in the scene approvingly. *There's nothin' primitive about this place,* she acknowledged privately. Aloud, she said, "Looks like Mrs. Bennett is airin' things out today. May be doin' some spring cleanin'."

From the start, MaryAnn took to Cora Bennett. Of medium height and build, Cora had a round face that was more pleasant than pretty. She laughed easily and her hazel eyes twinkled as she talked. Her calico dress and the apron covering it were as spotless as the kitchen in which they stood.

She greeted MaryAnn like an old friend and MaryAnn knew at once that Jubal had been right—Cora Bennett could never seem like a stranger. What's more, she had room enough to spare for all the Chidesters. As Cora ushered MaryAnn into the front door and through the hallway to the kitchen, MaryAnn glimpsed two large sitting rooms on either side of the hall. She assumed there must be at least three, probably four, bedrooms on the second floor. Suddenly, she felt ashamed that her pride had kept them all crowded in Jubal's tiny cabin when they could have been so comfortable in the Bennett home.

Cora motioned for MaryAnn to sit down at the table in the center of the large, sunny kitchen. "I'm cleanin' some greens," she explained, sitting in the next chair. "Must be a peck or more. Just gathered them this mornin'. I'll fix you a bunch to take home with you."

The basket of wild greens sat on the floor between them. Cora filled a pan from the basket and began to sort them, throwing the culls into an old bucket as she worked. Mary-Ann grabbed an empty pan and joined Cora in her work. Anxious to learn about Dogwood Creek, she kept her new acquaintance busy with questions.

"Why did you and Mr. Bennett come here, Cora? You fancy the frontier life?" MaryAnn asked, as relaxed as if she had known Cora all her life.

"Mercy, MaryAnn! This ain't the frontier. The frontier's clean passed us by. This is just a place where people come to get away from somethin'. For us it was the big plantations. We couldn't compete with the rich landowners who ran their farms with slave labor."

"Did you and your husband homestead this place?"

"Oh yes. Most folks around these parts did. Except for the Robins who flat out bought their land from some homesteader that up and left."

"I think we passed their place. They the ones that raise horses?"

"Umhmm. That's them." Cora dumped her picked-over greens into the large bowl on the table.

"I thought I saw some slaves there," MaryAnn commented.

"They do keep a few. And the Carricks at the mill, they have a few."

"Are they from the South?"

"Fact is, the Robins come here from England. They don't mingle much. Pretty genteel for the rest of us. But they're nice folk. They just keep to themselves—most people do. Now the Carricks, they come from over in the next county. Lived in Missouri all their lives."

The sound of wagon wheels on the road interrupted their conversation. Cora walked to the kitchen door. "It's the Millers—Pete and Cassie," she announced. "Cassie'll be along. I'll just wait here for her."

A few minutes later a tall, wiry woman greeted Cora at the door. Her dark calico dress matched her brown hair that was pulled back in a tight bun at the nape of her neck. Round wire glasses perched on a rather long nose and she squinted through them as she spoke to Cora. "We're goin' to Carricks for supplies," she called in a rather shrill voice. "Kin we bring you'uns anythin'?"

"I'm obliged, Cassie," Cora answered. "I'll make out a list."

Cassie nodded, then peered through her spectacles at MaryAnn. "You must be Mrs. Chidester," she greeted her. She pulled up a chair and grabbed another pan of greens. "I met your man at the barn." Then, ignoring the greens, she blurted out, "I heard you was stayin' with that Tate man what's cuttin' timber on yonder ridge."

Later, MaryAnn would wonder how it ever happened that she told Cassie so much about their plans, for she didn't much take to her. Perhaps it was because MaryAnn was determined to be neighborly, or perhaps it was simply that Cassie, unlike Cora, asked a lot of questions. For whatever reason, MaryAnn found herself telling Cassie that they were homesteading over on the ridge. She described their plans just as William John had spoken them.

Cora had rejoined them, list in hand, when Cassie interrupted the description. "Ye cain't mean on Solomon's Ridge." She stared at MaryAnn, mouth agape, as she tucked Cora's list into her apron pocket.

"You know the place?" MaryAnn asked.

"Ye cain't mean your man's fixin' to build a cabin in that place?" Cassie asked again.

"It seems to be a right nice place for a home," MaryAnn ventured, a bit defensively. Her hands worked nervously over the greens. *I might have my own quarrel with William John,* she thought angrily, *but I won't sit still and listen to some stranger pickin' fault with him and his plans.*

"Mind ye, I'll not argue thet," Cassie replied, "but if it wuz me, I'd be lookin' elsewhere. I wouldn't want no home 'thin earshot of thet haunted oak tree." Cassie shivered as she mentioned the tree.

"Haunted?!"

Cora moved closer and tried to stop the flow of Cassie's words. "Now Cassie, don't be scarin' MaryAnn with your tales." She removed the untouched pan of greens from Cassie's lap and settled back to clean them.

"I want to hear, Cora," MaryAnn spoke decidedly.

Cora shrugged. "Cassie'd probably tell you even if you don't." She gave MaryAnn a sideways glance of apology.

Cassie licked her lips and continued her tale. "Old Matt Reese found a man hung from the limb of thet oak with a note stuck in his belt. Don't rightly recall the exact words but it 'pears as if the dead man stole somebody's horse and brung it here, thinkin' to excape. But the owner, he tracked him down and tied a rope 'round his neck and hung him from a limb." Cassie waved her hands wildly as she talked. Then she clasped her fingers around her neck, demonstrating a choking motion.

She leaned in toward MaryAnn, adjusted her spectacles and continued her tale. "Word has it thet he set the thief atop the very horse he stole and run the horse out from under him. Then the owner, he taken his horse and went back where he come from and all the while thet there horse thief jist kep a hangin' on thet oak tree. Old Doc Mason over at the county seat calculated the dead man wuz hangin' there nigh a week 'fore Matt Reese happened by. Musta been a turrible sight. . . ."

Cassie ranted on about stinking dead corpses and ghosts come back to haunt the tree, but MaryAnn only half heard. Suddenly she felt ill. Her mind raced with questions. *Could*

Cassie's tale be true? Was that how William John came upon the perfect place for her home? Her husband had killed a man! William John had actually killed a man over that fool horse. She looked about, desperate to escape Cassie's chatter. Perhaps a drink from the water bucket—maybe she could even wet the corner of her apron and wipe her face. She felt so hot!

She stood up quickly, dumping her pan of greens to the floor. "Oh, Cora, I'm sorry. I'm that clumsy." She dropped to her knees and began picking up the greens.

It was then that she first noticed the shadow across the open kitchen door. She looked up and there stood her husband. His expression told her that he had heard everything.

"We'd best be going, MaryAnn." He waited for her to get up. Then, nodding toward the two women he said, "Likely we'll see you soon, Cora—Cassie." With that, he gripped MaryAnn's elbow firmly and guided her out to the waiting wagon.

When they had seated themselves on the wagon, William John snapped the reins angrily. "Cassie Miller's a meddling old biddie!" he declared. He sat straight as a poker and fixed his eyes on the road.

MaryAnn gripped the pan of greens that Cora had thrust into her hands. The shock of a moment ago had turned to a dull ache, and now to anger. She jammed the pan further into her lap as she responded to William John's words. "Cassie might be a meddlin' biddie, but I got from her what my own husband wouldn't tell me!"

William John snapped the reins again, urging the horses on as he flung back, "What you got from her was a bushel full of tittle-tattle!"

"Don't pretend with me any longer, William John. Ever since you come over to Missouri to fetch that fool horse, you've been as tight-lipped as a kid with a green persimmon. I told George before we left Indiana that somethin' was botherin' you. I told him I hardly knew you anymore. But I never dreamed you'd killed a man over that horse." MaryAnn's voice caught with a sob. She bit her lip to stop the pouring out of words. Furiously, she dabbed her hand at her eyes to stop the unwelcome tears.

"You can't believe that I killed a man!" William John exclaimed. He looked at her now, his eyes searching her face.

"What am I s'posed to believe? You heard Cassie tellin' the whole story."

"I didn't kill that man," William John said matter-of-factly.

"But you *did* find your horse there on the ridge," MaryAnn argued. "I could tell the day we came to that oak tree, and you . . . you say you didn't kill him?"

"I thought you knew me better than that, MaryAnn." Disappointment edged William John's voice.

"Then who . . . ?" Her dark eyes grew wide. "Not Jubal?"

"No, as Almighty God is my witness. I'd swear on my papa's Bible. Jubal and I had nothing to do with that killing." He spat the words out, clearly irritated by the conversation.

Then, calling the team to a halt, he wound the reins over his hand and settled on the seat beside MaryAnn. He drew a deep breath as he looked at her once more. "I reckon it's time I told you what happened."

"Long past time," she retorted.

"Do you aim to listen or just keep interrupting?" he snapped back.

"I'm listenin'," MaryAnn replied quietly. She turned her face up to him, ready to hear the secret he had kept for so many weeks.

"Jubal and I tracked my horse for five days or more. From the tracks, Jubal reckoned it was one man on a horse and one horse without a rider. Then about the sixth morning, the tracks showed three horses—two without riders according to Jubal's calculations. By afternoon of the next day we came upon a fourth set of tracks, a big horse with a rider—even I could tell that. By that time we were gaining on my horse pretty good, but we couldn't guess what might be going on with all those tracks."

He glanced up momentarily at a blue jay flitting among the trees that shaded the road. MaryAnn followed his gaze. For as far as they could see, the canopy of trees hung over the road. Ordinarily the simple beauty of such a scene would have commanded MaryAnn's attention. But not today. She urged William John to continue his story.

He licked his lips and began again. "All along we figured to overtake the horse thief at night when he was asleep and just take my horse and be gone. I never aimed to shoot a man to get my horse back."

"But you did?"

"Of course not!" William John shook his head impatiently at the interruption. "If you'll just listen, I'll tell you everything. The last day we were tracking we could tell that the lone rider on the big horse was getting closer. All the tracks looked fresh, but we were still pretty sure the big horse and the horse thief weren't traveling together. Then about nightfall we heard loud voices and we reckoned we had caught up with the lot. Jubal and I dismounted and hid behind some thick tree trunks. We could see two men. One was really big. He threw a rope about the other man's neck. Then he held a gun on him and put him astride the horse—"

"Your horse?" MaryAnn couldn't help asking.

"No, one of the others. We weren't sure what was happening of course, but we think the thief who took my horse must have also helped himself to one that belonged to the big man. Jubal and I didn't know what to do. We were afraid to take on a big angry man with a gun in his hand. So we just kept still."

"You watched the hangin'?" gasped MaryAnn.

"That's right." William John looked troubled as he spoke. He paused a moment, as if recalling the scene. Then, shaking his head slightly, he continued. "Just about the time the horse ran out from under the thief, I stepped on a loose rock. Jubal managed to hold our horses quiet, but the rolling rock made quite a racket. We knew the big man heard it because he stopped and stood real quiet for a minute. Then he just jumped on his horse, grabbed the reins of the other horses, and galloped out of there."

"He grabbed your horse too?" MaryAnn asked, a look of confusion on her face. "How did you get him back?"

"No, no! He was standing loose, not even tethered, and I whistled to him low like I always call him. He jerked his head up and whinnied. Right then, the big man galloped away. Jubal figured the man knew my horse had just heard its owner and that if he didn't get out he might be accused of stealing it and end up like the man he just hanged." William John rubbed his chin thoughtfully as he finished. "That's the real story, MaryAnn."

She studied his face and pondered the horror of her husband's experience. Almost in a whisper, she said, "It musta been a terrible thing to see." A look of sympathy crossed her face as she continued. "But what I don't understand is, why couldn't you tell me all that before now?"

"MaryAnn, I watched that man hang. Jubal and I didn't even cut him down. We just rode hard out of there. It all happened so fast, we didn't know what to do—except to grab my horse and get out. We didn't fancy ending up on that limb ourselves."

MaryAnn nodded in understanding. It was like her husband to be troubled over anything so violent as a hanging— even if it were a horse thief who had taken William John's own horse. She patted his hand lightly. The gesture encouraged him to continue.

"We stayed on Dogwood Creek for nearly a week after that. We met Logan Bennett at Carrick's Mill, and Logan invited us to sleep in his barn. At first we didn't tell him what had happened. We were afraid he might think we had done it ourselves. But after two days I couldn't stand it; I felt we had to go back and give the man a decent burial."

"You went back after two days?" Mary stopped her husband with a tug at his sleeve.

"That's right. The third morning Jubal and I rode back together, but the body was gone."

"Cassie said the body had hung nearly a week."

"Cassie exaggerates," he said emphatically. "It couldn't have hung more than forty-eight hours. We went back to the Bennetts', and I told Logan what had happened."

"And he believed you?"

"Yes, he did. It seems some people over at the county seat had talked to a big man looking for a stranger leading two extra horses. They put the whole thing together before I ever told Logan."

"I could tell that Lee William and Russell knew somethin' the day we came to the ridge," said MaryAnn, her lips pursed. "And you just told me that the Bennetts knew all about it. How come it was so hard to tell me what the rest of them already knew, William John?" She looked intently at her husband, a hint of urgency in her quietly spoken words.

William John lifted the reins and the wagon jolted to a start again. Above the noise of the wheels, he offered an explanation. "MaryAnn, when I told you about Dogwood Creek, the first thing you said was it sounded too primitive. I figured you'd never agree to come if I told you that story. But the day we went back to see about the body I got a look at that spot just below the ridge. We even drank at the spring. It was so beautiful, I knew that once you saw it . . ." His voice trailed off and he shook his head as if remembering his first glimpse of the spot.

A sudden relief washed over MaryAnn as William John spoke. All the uncertainty of the past weeks slipped away. She closed her eyes and saw the place that William John had chosen for her. She knew that together, with no more secrets between them, she and William John would make a new home. She sat quietly, searching for the right words. Then she placed her hand over his on the reins and said softly, "I'm glad you told me, William John. Next time don't wait so long."

"I wanted to tell you when it was just you and me. But it seems like we haven't been alone since we got here. I hated to admit to you how afraid I was that night when we got my horse back. A man ought not to fear . . . especially if he has a woman to take care of."

His words touched MaryAnn, and she felt easy again about the two of them. She slid closer to him on the wagon seat,

63

taking care not to spill the pan of greens resting in her lap. She tucked her hand under William John's arm and squeezed it gently. "You're a right good husband, William John, and you've always taken good care of me. I expect that's not goin' to change after all these years."

"I've had help, MaryAnn. I believe the Almighty is watching out for us, and that's what I expect is never going to change."

MaryAnn's eyes nearly filled with tears again. It was so like William John to say that. He depended on God in a way that MaryAnn almost envied. William John's plans and dreams were always wrapped up in the Almighty, and he counted on God to watch out for them. MaryAnn, unlike her husband, usually found it easier to trust in her own hard work than to trust in the God she couldn't see. She prayed to the Almighty, for she believed in Him deeply. But there was a distance between her and her Maker, a distance that William John obviously never felt. She wondered whether she would ever come to trust God the way William John did.

William John pulled the team to a halt at Jubal's clearing. He tied up the reins and helped MaryAnn down, reaching first for the pan of greens. When she was safely on the ground he wrapped his arms around her waist briefly. Then they walked arm in arm toward Jubal's cabin.

"There's one more thing, Mrs. Chidester," said William John with a grin. "Tomorrow you'll have a house of your own. The Smiths are gone and we're going to their cabin first thing come morning."

"Tomorrow!" she exclaimed. Her eyes danced at the thought. Tomorrow she and William John would make a new start.

CHAPTER SEVEN

Politics

※

Lee William met his parents at the door of Jubal's cabin. In his hands he clasped a folded newspaper. MaryAnn glanced at it curiously as she walked by and set the pan of greens on the table. Russell and Jubal were seated at the table and Jubal's eyes widened at the sight of Cora's gift.

"Theeey! Ain't that purty!" he exclaimed, licking his lips in anticipation.

Lucy, seated on the bed, looked up from the tiny gown she was sewing. "I'll cook 'em up directly, Pa," she said. "It's almost dinner time." She glanced down at Arial playing on the floor and took up her sewing once more.

MaryAnn looked about the crowded room and felt again the anticipation of moving to the Smith cabin. But Lee William cut short her musing as he waved the newspaper in the air. "We've been to Carrick's Mill," he said. "Mr. Carrick gave us this paper. It says here that a new bill, the Kansas Nebraska Act, is about to be signed into law. Says that when it's signed, the Missouri Compromise will be repealed and the slavery question in Kansas will be decided by the people."

"I coulda told you that wuz comin', Lee William," Jubal volunteered. "Thet's why the Smiths is aimin' to leave."

"They've gone, Jubal," William John said. "We're moving to their cabin tomorrow. But I thought they were moving closer to some of their family along the Missouri."

"They got family along the Missouri alright, but they're headin' fer Kansas. Aimin' to join the slavers and open the Territory to slavery," Jubal replied.

MaryAnn watched Lee William's jaw tighten as it always did when the question of slavery was raised. Normally her seventh son was as calm as a falling snow, but he fairly churned when somebody mentioned slavery. He looked at William John as he blurted out, "Pa, I don't aim to be obliged to any slavers. I don't fancy moving to a cabin left behind by people bound to open another state to slavery."

"It's only a cabin, Lee William," said Russell.

"Don't be so hotheaded, boy," Jubal remonstrated, slapping Lee William on the back. "I'd be proud to hev you and Lucy stay s'long as you want, but you're on Dogwood Creek now. Best hold your tongue."

"What are you trying to say, Jubal?"

"Jist that folks don't all have the same politics, but they's good neighbors. Reckon there's no room on the Creek for those what ain't."

William John studied his son intently before he spoke. "Well, Son, you can decide for yourself. Your Ma and I, and probably Russell—we're going first thing tomorrow." Then, turning to MaryAnn, he said, "I forgot to tell you. The Smith's oldest boy, James, will be around for a month yet. Seems he had hired out to Mr. Robin in exchange for a saddle horse. Do you mind having him around? Logan says he plans to bunk in the barn."

"I've had seven sons—I'm used to having boys around!" she said agreeably. She saw William John relax. "Does he plan to follow his folks to Kansas when he leaves?" she asked.

William John shrugged and looked at Jubal. "Logan didn't say. Jubal, what about young James? You think he'll follow his folks to Kansas?"

"I'm sartin of thet." Jubal picked up Arial and began to bounce her on his knee. "The whole Smith family is bound to aid the cause of slavery in Kansas."

"Well they may have a battle," Lee William broke in. "Look here." He directed his remarks to William John as he pointed to an article in the newspaper. "The paper says that a new town called Lawrence is being founded by some parties sent by the New England Emigrant Aid Society. And this society is planning to send more. They'll not give over the Territory easy-like to a bunch of slavers," he finished defiantly.

"No, likely not, Lee William. They'll just all get into a royal scrap and your hotheaded abolitionist friends'll split Kansas apart before it ever becomes a state." As usual, Russell saw the situation differently from his brother. Unlike Lee William, Russell spoke matter-of-factly on the question, betraying no emotion.

"Well, boys, we're not going to settle this question tonight," William John interjected. "We'd better be discussing our plans for settling in. How'd the clearing go today?"

MaryAnn smiled to herself about the easy way her husband turned the discussion. William John didn't take to heated debates of any kind. They made him uncomfortable. He especially disliked arguments over the country's political problems. While he didn't approve of slavery, he considered it a question better left for others to debate. Whenever Lee William and Russell got on the subject, as they frequently

67

did, William John always found a way to divert their attention elsewhere.

Russell answered William John's question with a shrug. "It's going slow, Pa." He and Lee William had spent every day clearing a quarter-acre field on Solomon's Ridge. "It's going to take some time," Russell added. "I can't see how we can get enough cleared to make a decent crop this year." He tugged at his limp arm. There was an edge of worry in his voice, and MaryAnn realized that he was counting on the family getting well settled this first season. *He's that anxious to get on to his job in Carondolet,* she thought.

"Never mind, boys," said their father. "Logan tells me that Smith had cleared nearly five acres, and he didn't plant anything this year. We can use the land. We're too late for oats—they tell me they get killing frost by the middle of September some years. But we'll put in corn and sorghum. We'll plow there tomorrow. I'll take your mama to the Smith cabin first thing and unload the wagon. Then I'll be along with the plow and the team."

"Make that Mama and Lucy, Pa," Lee William cut in. "I reckon I wasn't thinking." He gazed fondly at his larger-than-usual wife, and she returned his smile, her blue eyes glistening. She rose stiffly from the bed and came to stand next to him.

MaryAnn felt a surge of pride as she looked at her strong, handsome son and his attractive wife with hair the color of young corn. The Smith cabin would be comfortable for Lucy as she awaited the birth of her child. And MaryAnn looked forward to the company of her daughter-in-law and young Arial.

They were very different—Lucy and MaryAnn. Lucy went happily about her indoor work, begrudging every minute spent on chores outside her home. MaryAnn found every excuse to let the inside work go so that she could be outside, drinking in the sunshine and the fragrance of the season as she worked in the soil.

Quiet by nature, Lucy always seemed to know just what to say—or not to say. MaryAnn, strongwilled and outspoken most of the time, found that words failed her when she most needed them.

The three older Chidester sons had married after they moved to Missouri and MaryAnn had never met their wives. MaryAnn always thought of Lucy as her only daughter-in-law.

From the start, she admired Lucy's fetching ways. Lucy always filled her house with wildflowers—sometimes stuck in a jar, sometimes arranged with wet moss in a hollowed-out gourd. She covered her and Lee William's bed with one of her most delicately patterned quilts. Once MaryAnn had over-heard an astonished neighbor woman remark that the quilt was far too nice to serve as an everyday covering. And Lucy had answered softly that she made it for Lee William and didn't fancy hiding it away in a trunk.

The first spring after Lucy married Lee William, she persuaded the family to celebrate Johnny-Jump-Up Day. She appeared at MaryAnn's door just ahead of supper announcing, "I found my first johnny-jump-ups today and I baked this here simnel cake to celebrate." Later when the family gathered around the table, they thought it almost too pretty to eat with its white icing and candied wild violets on top. When they had tasted it they declared at once that johnny-jump-up day must be celebrated every spring with a simnel cake from Lucy's oven.

MaryAnn looked at Lucy, standing at the cookstove now, preparing drippings and vinegar for the greens. She had no doubts—she and Lucy would do well living together in the Smith cabin.

Jubal stood up, holding Arial in his arms. "They ain't room in here fer a decent dog fight," he remarked. "I'll take the young'un outside while you're cookin'." The men followed him through the open door.

An instant later, Jubal ducked his head back in the cabin. "I'll go along to the Smith cabin with you womenfolk tomorrow," he volunteered. "I kin chop some wood and carry water. I know it takes a powerful lot of water when a woman decides to scrub a house." His eyes twinkled as he added, "Many's the day Lucy's kep' me busy totin' water—startin' from time she wasn't much bigger'n Arial!"

"Oh Pa! There you go again. Don't you never stop exaggeratin'?" Lucy protested. She grabbed a dishtowel and swiped at him. "If you want greens with your dinner, you'd better scoot outta here now." Jubal chuckled and edged out the door.

MaryAnn laughed with Lucy. Impulsively, she hugged the younger woman and said, "Tomorrow we'll have more room for cookin' our dinner."

Lucy smiled. "I'm that glad Lee William decided to go with you," she said softly.

———

MaryAnn was pleasantly surprised with the Smith cabin—it was not nearly so nice as her home in Indiana nor as comfortable as the Bennetts', but it was certainly better than Jubal's hastily built one-room one.

She found the kitchen to be the largest of the three rooms, taking up half of the cabin. The remaining half was divided to make two bedrooms. A small sleeping loft could be reached from the kitchen. MaryAnn stood beneath the pole ladder that led to the loft. Nailed to the kitchen side of the cabin's center wall, it showed little sign of use. "Not so good for a one-armed man," MaryAnn mused, knowing that Russell would be the one to use the loft. Unaware that she had spoken aloud, she was startled to hear Lucy say, "Russell won't have no trouble with thet. You don't need to worry."

MaryAnn sighed. "You're right, Lucy. He'll be fine. It's just . . . I guess a mother never stops worrying." Turning away from the wall she eyed the few pieces of furniture left by the Smiths. A large plank table and two long benches sat in the middle of the kitchen. At the far end stood the cookstove, still hooked to its smokepipe. An empty woodbox stood nearby. MaryAnn walked to the stove and gingerly ran a finger across the top. It could do with some scrubbing, but right now she needed a fire built in it.

As if anticipating her needs, Jubal came through the door with a load of kindling. While he fussed over starting a fire, MaryAnn and Lucy inspected the bedrooms. One opened to the outside, the other opened to the kitchen—and there was a door between the two bedrooms. MaryAnn thought longingly of the arrangement of the Brean log house and vowed to remind William John to include a hallway in their new home. In the meantime they would all put up with the inconvenience of a cabin built without one.

The first bedroom was bare, but in the second they found a bed, like Jubal's, built out from the wall. MaryAnn passed by the bed and flung the door open. "We'll air things out," she said, then stepped outside, intent on getting another look at their temporary home.

71

The unhewn logs were carefully chinked and daubed.

"It looks like a real tight cabin," said Lucy, following along with Arial toddling beside her.

MaryAnn agreed. "We'll be warm enough come winter, I expect."

They walked around the house where the kitchen door opened onto a small porch. MaryAnn's trunk sat on one end of the porch, with the rest of their belongings piled beside. MaryAnn glanced at the pile, remembering that it had taken William John hardly any time at all to unload it. She noted once again that it was a scanty bunch of belongings. But the thought did not trouble her this morning, for to the west of the house she spied a good-sized garden plot. She paused in her inspection, gazing at the plot. Then, she grabbed her broom from the pile, turned to Lucy and said, "I'd best get on with my cleanin'. I want to finish today so I'll have time for the garden tomorrow."

In the kitchen, they found the stove already hot from Jubal's fire. As he adjusted the damper slightly, Jubal volunteered, "I'll be fetchin' that copper boiler from the porch now an' fillin' it with water."

MaryAnn insisted that Lucy take it easy and put her to work cooking up some provisions for the evening meal. The men would not be home for the noon dinner.

Jubal split a week's supply of wood and filled both the woodbox and the kindling box in the kitchen. He came in and out throughout the day, filling water buckets and the copper boiler. He helped MaryAnn move the few things they had brought in the wagon. First, they brought the rockers—the only two chairs that William John and MaryAnn owned. She placed them in the corner of the kitchen.

MaryAnn unpacked the trunk—still sitting on the porch—while Jubal brought in the baskets of kitchen things. Next Jubal nailed some shelves on the walls. He put two behind the stove and one across the room for the clock William John had given MaryAnn on their wedding day. MaryAnn positioned the clock on the shelf. Beside it she lay William John's Bible, the only thing left to him by his father. On the same wall, away from the smoke and grease of cooking, she hung Great-grandma Brean's painting. She stood back a moment and scrutinized the effect. After adjusting the rockers she asked Jubal to bring the now empty trunk and place it along the wall between the two chairs. "It'll work well for settin' things on," she explained.

MaryAnn distributed the quilts in the well-scrubbed bedrooms. Remembering how stiff her own joints had become during her pregnancies, she took the feather tick to the second room and placed it on the crude bed to give Lucy more comfort. In the other room she made a pallet of quilts on the floor for her and William John.

Jubal carried quilts to the loft for Russell's pallet. He left before supper, and MaryAnn heard Lucy tell him that they would be back on the next day.

For an instant, MaryAnn wondered if Lucy might be uncomfortable about moving in with her husband's parents. She looked at her daughter-in-law questioningly. "You're right welcome to stay with us, you know, Lucy."

"Yes ma'am. I know that. It's jist that I ain't seen my pa in so long and he's enjoyin' Arial so. We talked on it, me and Lee William, and iffen it's alright with you'uns, we'll be stayin' with Pa another month. But we reckoned we best move in with you for my confinement time."

MaryAnn nodded in understanding. It was like Lucy to think of Jubal before her own comfort.

———————

The evening shadows had begun to fall before the men came in. MaryAnn had scrubbed the table and covered it with a cloth. She was lighting the lamp when William John's voice boomed from the doorway, "Mrs. Chidester!" His voice betrayed no weariness from the long day's work. He stomped off some field mud from his boots and came quickly into the room. Casting his eyes about the cabin, he remarked with mock formality, "I see you've been busy, ma'am!" He threw his hat in the corner, rolled up his sleeves, and scrubbed himself at the wash basin.

"We've both been busy. Come and eat." It was not MaryAnn's way to talk about such things, but she was pleased that her husband had noted her efforts to make a home in this unfamiliar place.

"Looks like you got it all done," he commented.

"Wasn't that much to do—just scrubbin'. Didn't take long to unpack one trunk and lay out quilts."

"We'll get you some furniture soon." He came to her and laid his hand gently on her shoulder.

"No need," MaryAnn said decidedly. "We'd just have to move it. We can make do until we get in our own cabin." A part of MaryAnn longed for a few more furnishings in the sparse cabin. But she knew the men had no time to make furniture or to drive the wagon around to collect such pieces as might be found at sales. There would be time for that later. Right now the men had fields to sow and she had a garden to plant.

She explained further to William John, "Tomorrow I aim to start puttin' in the garden. Mrs. Smith had a right nice plot. It just has to be hoed and planted."

William John smiled. "I know, MaryAnn," he said teasingly. "You'd rather have a garden to work than a houseful of furniture to dust."

MaryAnn returned his smile. "Right now, I'd just like some menfolk to come and eat."

They were still sitting at the table after supper when the Smith's boy, James, came to the door. He stood there for a moment, hat in hand, and explained who he was. MaryAnn insisted that he sit and eat a bit.

In the lamplight she studied his small, thin frame. His straight blond hair hung to the collar of his course homespun shirt. He darted his eyes about nervously at first, then held them on his plate, as if he were uncomfortable sitting next to the three men.

He looks so young next to Russell and Lee William, MaryAnn thought. *He's just a boy! Not even shavin' yet. He's got no business goin' off to the Kansas border!* Aloud she said, "Now you come and eat with us as long as you're here. It's the least we can do for the use of the cabin."

"Don't reckon we have any use for the cabin anymore, ma'am," he said respectfully. "The folks, they don't aim to come back to Dogwood Creek. They're glad somebody kin use it."

He glanced about the table hungrily, having sopped his plate clean. At MaryAnn's urging, he filled his plate once more. " . . . mighty good victuals, Mrs. Chidester," he said appreciatively.

MaryAnn smiled, but explained quickly that the young Mrs. Chidester—Lucy—had cooked the meal.

Even Lee William seemed to take to the polite young man with the thick Southern drawl, and MaryAnn was glad to see that in the way of Dogwood Creek, her family was able to be neighborly—in spite of political differences.

It was after James left, insisting that he would be sleeping each night in the barn, that Russell brought up the Kansas situation again.

"I read that the New England people are bound to claim Kansas as free soil. Henry Ward Beecher is encouraging hundreds of them to come. He's even furnishing everyone with a Bible and a rifle. What do you make of that, Pa?"

"I can't see that Almighty God is pleased with such goings on," answered William John quietly.

MaryAnn rose from the table and began to clear away the dirty dishes. From the corner of her eye she saw Lee William squirming uneasily in his chair.

"I never figured God to be on the side of slavers, Pa," Lee William declared. "It can't be right for one man to own another, no matter what color his skin."

MaryAnn turned her head sharply, expecting the inevitable debate. But Russell spoke kindly as he leaned toward his younger brother, and raised the next question. "You reckon God is on the side of the rifle-packing, Bible-toting abolitionists?"

"Russell, sometimes you sound like you'd as soon let the slavers have their own way. Don't you believe slavery ought to be abolished?" Lee William queried.

"Truth is, I do. I'm certain it should be abolished. But I'm not sure how it should be done. I don't believe a man ought to own another man, any more than you do. But I'm not ready to destroy the Union to bring about abolition."

Russell paused briefly, peering deeply into his brother's eyes. "I see war coming, Lee William, and I'm afraid people are going to be fighting among themselves. It won't all be because they're so fired up to set the slaves free. I'm afraid we're not likely to have a union of states left if we're not careful. Think on that a spell, Little Brother. The Union is what gives the country strength. Something tells me that whatever happens, we've got to preserve that Union."

"You're right, Russell," William John observed. "And the best way to do that is for everybody to mind their own business. We got no cause to fight any war in Kansas. This is Dogwood Creek, and I don't reckon it's going to affect us here."

MaryAnn saw Russell open his mouth as if to argue William John's point. Instead he shrugged, stood up, and said, "I reckon I'll turn in, Ma. Which one of those fancy beds has my name on it?"

MaryAnn breathed a sigh of relief that once again William John had diverted the argument before it disrupted the peace in their home.

CHAPTER EIGHT

Heart's Desire

—— ≈ ——

From the start, it was plain to MaryAnn that William John had found all that he was looking for on Dogwood Creek. While she was glad for him, she often felt that his deep contentment made him unaware of her own struggles.

For MaryAnn, the first winter was the hardest. She longed for her Indiana home with its space and its cozy fireplace. The Smith cabin with neither hallway nor fireplace proved to be a daily reminder of all she had left behind. Only the birth of Amy, Lee William and Lucy's new baby girl, made the winter more tolerable.

Amy was born late in September with both MaryAnn and William John attending. William John had attended all the Chidester birthings. He had learned midwifery from his doctor father and had in turn taught MaryAnn. She had often wondered whether William John would have been a doctor if his father had not been killed in a runaway buggy. But she had never asked, for her husband thought it foolish to speculate about what might have been.

On the morning that Lucy felt the birth pangs, Russell took charge of his young niece, Arial. He set her astride William John's saddle horse and, squeezing in behind her, rode across the ridge to Jubal Tate's cabin. They stayed the night with Jubal. The next morning, all three returned for their first look at the new baby.

After the first snow fell, MaryAnn found more time to rock little Amy. Day after day, as she cuddled the infant closely and looked through the window at the whitened landscape, she wished for an early spring. Perhaps in spring, the beauty of Dogwood Creek would take away some of the homesickness she felt for Indiana.

Her spirits lifted on those evenings when Lee William brought out Ian Brean's fiddle. Everyone sat around the kitchen while the two boys played all the old favorite tunes. Arial would climb up on William John's lap and snuggle down into her grandpa's arms. Seeing everyone looking so content, MaryAnn had to admit that at times winter was not so bad.

During that first winter, with the help of Lee William and Russell, William John cut enough logs to build their house. When they were done cutting, Logan Bennett came with froe and mallet to help make the roof shingles. William John selected several logs and cut them into two-foot lengths. Then, standing one of the cut logs on end, he drove a wooden wedge deep into the trunk. With his maul, he drove the wedge deeper and deeper until the log split in half. Logan then showed them how to turn the half log into shingles. He split the half into four equal wedges. After cutting the heartwood away, he split each wedge into four thick boards. Choosing one of the boards, Logan walked to the board brake he had set up nearby. It was made from the narrow crotch of a black gum tree and it held the board in place while Logan rived out the shingles. Holding the froe firmly against the end of the board, he struck it sharply with the mallet, splitting the board in two. Soon a pile of shingles lay nearby.

Seeing Logan's expert work, the men quickly decided to divide the labor in such a way that Logan could rive all the shingles. William John and Lee William cut the logs, split the wedges and made the thick boards. Russell carried the boards to Logan and stacked the finished shingles for curing.

In the spring, after the first plowing was done, all the neighbors came to raise the Chidester cabin. Even the Millers came—although Cassie still insisted that the oak tree on the ridge was haunted.

William John partitioned the cabin three ways, making a large kitchen across one end. Both the front and back door opened to the kitchen. Next to the kitchen was the parlor, with a window and another door facing the walnut tree and the spring beyond. The third room, partitioned off the parlor, was the bedroom. On the backside of the cabin, the bedroom window gave a clear view of Solomon's Ridge and the great oak tree. Above the parlor William John made a loft room for sleeping. Like the downstairs bedroom, the loft was big enough for two beds. He built a sturdy stairway to the loft, saying that no one should have to climb to the room on a ladder.

MaryAnn told William John that it was a fine house and never once acknowledged that it was smaller than their previous home with George. While she had hoped for a hallway, she could see that William John had laid out the house so well they would not need one.

Russell stayed on Dogwood Creek long enough to see the cabin built. But before MaryAnn and William John moved in, he left for St. Louis. MaryAnn wondered if Russell's stay on Dogwood Creek had been cut short because of all the political problems in the country. Even though Russell had planned all along to go to St. Louis, he left almost without warning. The three men had debated the Kansas situation the night before and Lee William had angrily denounced his brother's more moderate views. The next morning Russell left before breakfast, telling MaryAnn to say his good-byes for him when the men came in from milking. A week later, a letter came to Carrick's Mill, saying that he had found a job at the shipyards in Carondolet.

On the same day the letter arrived, MaryAnn and William John stood under the walnut tree looking at the finished, but still empty cabin. The tightly shingled roof not only covered the house but the front porch as well. William John had insisted that the porch run the width of the cabin, and that it be properly covered. Now he caught MaryAnn by the hand and drew her onto the porch. He turned her to face the tree and waved his hand at the landscape before them. From right to left, he pointed to the little south field, the spring-fed creek, and the row of sycamore trees.

"When it's hot this summer," he said, "we can sit out here in the evening and look at all this while we listen to the whippoorwills." His eyes shone with excitement as he looked from MaryAnn to the view and back to her.

MaryAnn, catching some of her husband's eagerness, pressed him to move at once. "Can't we load the wagon first thing in the mornin'?" she asked. "We could be in our own home this time tomorrow." To her surprise, he hesitated. Then, smiling mysteriously, he said that he couldn't spare the wagon tomorrow and they would have to wait one more day.

On the day they moved, William John acted as excited as a kid with a new calf. At the cabin, he helped her down and hurried her to the house, flinging the door wide open in front of her. MaryAnn gasped in surprise. The parlor was full of furniture. Eagerly, William John grabbed her by the hand and dragged her from room to room. MaryAnn's eyes glistened with tears as she found each successive room furnished.

"Two more families left Dogwood Creek for Kansas Territory," William John explained. "I bought all this from them. That's why I needed the wagon—to go gather it up and haul it here."

She looked around the parlor once more and her eyes came to rest on the fireplace that William John had made. "There's only one thing this room needs," she said, staring at a place above the mantel.

William John disappeared at once. In a moment he was back, the picture of Great-grandmother Brean in hand. "Would you be meaning this?" he asked with a twinkle in his eyes.

MaryAnn's eyes brightened as she replied, "Please, William John, can you hang it this minute? I can't wait to see it above the mantel."

When he had hung the painting, they stood back a few steps and studied the picture. William John took MaryAnn's hand in his own and asked quietly, "Does it seem more like home to you now?"

She squeezed his hand in response, but she could not speak. A vision of her brother came to her and she wished that George could be with them now. She wished that he could see her in her new home, with Great-grandmother Brean's picture hanging above the fireplace. She thought about the empty wall above George's fireplace and wondered whether her brother would ever bring their Irish kin to Indiana.

A year later, in 1856, MaryAnn still remembered her first feeling of having a cabin of their own, with all they needed to make it a home. With the magic of May settling on her once more, she would walk through the rooms, rubbing her hands over the fine old furniture that William John had bought. And she never looked at the painting of Great-grandmother Brean without thinking of her brother George and his struggles to bring the rest of the Breans to America.

On this warm morning, as she made her way to her garden, she smiled wryly, recalling George's letter of a month ago. *So far, he's not havin' any more luck than our pa had,* she thought. She had said that very thing to William John that morning before he left for Carrick's Mill. Characteristically, William John had tried to encourage her. "It's time for another letter," he said. "Maybe there'll be one today."

As she pulled weeds from among the lettuce, she listened eagerly for the sound of William John's horse. She had come to the end of a long row of onions when the horse whinnied from down the lane. In a few minutes William John rode up to the garden gate. He dismounted quickly, tied the horse, and handed her a letter.

"I'll just get a drink from the kitchen and then I have to be going to the field," he said. He jerked his head toward the letter and added, "I told you there'd be a letter. Maybe George has good news this time."

He ducked into the house for his drink and was back before MaryAnn had finished the letter. "Listen to this, William John," she said excitedly, "I think George is about to have some company in that big house." She bit her lip, wishing she had not referred to the size of George's house, but William John seemed not to notice. "Read it to me," he said, leaning against the gate post.

She turned her back to the sun and began to read.

On Saturday last I heard from Sean Brean and he is eager to take advantage of my offer. He plans to come as far as New York when he has saved the passage fare. He hopes to work his way West on one of the river boats from there. Casey will come as soon afterward as possible.

MaryAnn paused and, shading her eyes with her hand, looked at William John. "Think of it!" she exclaimed. "They're comin' at long last."

"Does he say when they might come, MaryAnn?"

She read on.

Sean calculated that it might take him two years to raise the passage for New York.

MaryAnn sighed. "Two years! Why I thought he'd be comin' on the next boat."

William John laughed heartily. "You sound exactly like your mother, MaryAnn."

She laughed and admitted that he was right. When they had both quieted, she read the conclusion of George's letter.

I don't mind waiting two more years. After all, we've waited a lifetime already.

"He'll keep tryin'," MaryAnn said emphatically. "He always did. Once he decided to do somethin', he never gave up until he got it done."

William John nodded. "I remember the first time I met your brother, MaryAnn. He came riding into the village in that fancy Irish jaunting cart of his. When I admired it, he told me how he had made it. It didn't seem possible to me that a man could build something so complicated just from studying a painting. I knew right then that George Brean was the kind of man who would never give up easily on anything he had a mind to do."

As they talked, their eyes were drawn to a robin nearby. With feet planted firmly on the ground, the bird tugged stubbornly at an earthworm that was halfway under the ground. MaryAnn chuckled softly. "Papa used to say that George went after things like a spring robin after its dinner. He was always too stubborn to give up on anythin'. But of course he had help with the jauntin' cart, you know. Papa and George built that together."

She fingered the letter unconsciously and looked fondly at William John as she continued. "George and me—we was always starin' at Grandma Brean's picture, but for different reasons. He was studyin' the cart, and I was tryin' to imagine what life was like for that young girl in the cart. Now our

Papa, he never called it a cart. He said its proper name was an 'inside car.' "

William John leaned back against the post once more and crossed his arms. His eyes twinkled as he commented, "Well, whatever they called it, I'm glad they built it. Otherwise—"

"Otherwise you'd never have talked to George, let alone come home with him." MaryAnn finished the sentence, for she had heard him say it many times before. "I never paid any mind to George's friends before that. But when he came walkin' into the house and made you acquainted with Mama and me—well I knew right then I wanted to know more about William John Chidester. I could hardly believe my ears when you said you was lookin' for a temporary place to board. And when the teaching job opened, I thought I couldn't stand for you to go away."

She paused then as she always did at this point in her recollection of their first meeting. Looking a bit misty-eyed, she concluded, "And then the night before you left you asked me would I marry you and promised to come back the next summer."

William John touched her cheek with an uncommon gesture of gentleness. "And so you became Mrs. Chidester and now here you are, homesteading in the Ozarks!"

Again they laughed together. But MayAnn felt it a serious moment in her heart. It had taken a long lesson in trust—trust in her husband and trust in God—for her to learn that home was wherever she lived and loved and worked. It had been her husband's dream to have this place, and she had been loath to make it her own. But from the day they moved into their own house, MaryAnn had felt at home. Like William John, she had begun to feel they belonged on Dogwood Creek. Yet, in the year that they lived in their own cabin, she had never admitted these things to him. Now she felt an urge to tell William John that everything was as he had dreamed it would be.

"There's no place I'd rather be," she said, enthusiastically. "Especially in the month of May."

CHAPTER NINE

A Country Gone Crazy

———— ∾ ————

On the last day of the month, MaryAnn gathered dirty clothes into a hickory basket in preparation for washing. She hummed to herself, thinking all the while that May on Solomon's Ridge was unlike any other season or place. She even looked forward to washday.

She carried her basket of clothes to the kettle down by the spring. William John had filled the kettle with water, and built a fire under it before he left for the field. She tested the water carefully with her forefinger and, finding it the right temperature, began to shave soap into it. After splashing her hands through the water to dissolve the soap, she dumped in the first load of clothes and stirred them vigorously.

Left to herself, MaryAnn easily got lost in memories, especially when she was standing over a washboard. On this particular morning as she rubbed the soaked garments on the board, she pondered over all that had happened in the two years since they left Indiana. After they had moved into their new cabin, Lucy and Lee William continued to live in the Smith place, but they were getting ready to raise a cabin over on the ridge beyond the apple orchard. They expected to be in it before fall. *Too bad they couldn't have been there now,* MaryAnn thought, for Lucy was expecting her fifth child most any day. *It would be nice to have her closer.*

William John had already taught two terms of school. There was a new log schoolhouse at the head of Dogwood Creek, thanks to Logan Bennett who got the menfolk together to build it. William John had persuaded some of the young men on Dogwood Creek to attend the school along with the little boys. From the start, he showed special concern for those who had grown up on the creek with no school to attend. He was especially proud of his older students who had quickly mastered reading and writing.

After William John taught the first term, Logan persuaded him to hold Sunday meetings in the school twice every month. William John had protested, declaring that he was no preacher. Still he could see plain as day that Dogwood Creek needed one. So in time he had given in and had become the first preacher as well as the first schoolteacher to come to Dogwood Creek.

It seemed to MaryAnn that the more William John taught the Bible at the schoolhouse, the more his trust in the Almighty grew. There could be little doubt that this trust in turn added to William John's contentment. Oftentimes MaryAnn found herself wishing that some of her husband's contentment would rub off on their seventh son.

She wiped her hands on her apron and poked at the fire beneath the wash kettle. Then, grabbing one of William John's shirts, she rubbed it vigorously on the washboard. *We've a lot to be thankful for,* she thought. *All the same, there's always somethin' for a mother to worry about.*

Of late she worried about Lee William. He and Russell had quickly mended their quarrel through letters, but he had never quit stewing over the Kansas border problem. Somehow it seemed important to him to understand what side of the question God was on—a question he and Russell Brean had argued the first week they came to Dogwood Creek. Now, two years later, Lee William seemed to be more perplexed than ever.

It had been plain from the beginning that Lee William thought himself to be an abolitionist. For a long time he insisted that God could only be on the side of people who wanted to do away with the abominable practice of slavery.

And then John Brown came to Kansas.

MaryAnn reckoned that the change in Lee William had started then. He read everything he could find about Brown fighting the abolitionist cause in the Territory. The more he read, the more he brooded. If the newspapers could be believed, there wasn't much difference in the way abolitionists or slavers acted. One side or the other was always clubbing someone.

MaryAnn could tell that Lee William wasn't sure in his mind about the abolitionists anymore. For sure he didn't know what to make of that fiery old man who was making such a stir in Kansas. William John was no help at all when it came to their son's political concerns. His answer was always the same. "It doesn't concern us, Lee William. Dogwood Creek's a right safe place to raise a family so it's best we mind our own business."

MaryAnn wrung out the last of the overalls, tossed them into the basket, and doused the fire with a gourd full of washwater. Picking up the basket, she moved to the clothesline. As she hung the freshly washed garments, she checked the sun's position. *I s'pose it's time to get dinner for William John,* she mused. *And most likely Lee William will be along. Seems I heard he'd be workin' with his pa today.*

In the kitchen she stirred up the fire in the cookstove and laid out the table for three. She took two loaves of bread, baked fresh the day before, and tied a clean dish towel around them. *I'll send these home with Lee William,* she thought. *With Lucy's time almost come, she probably don't feel much like bakin'.* But when William John came in he was alone.

"Lee William didn't come to the field," he explained as MaryAnn set the victuals before him.

"It must be Lucy's time. We best eat and then I'll go check on her," MaryAnn volunteered.

"I'll be in the hilltop field if you need me," William John replied.

Their meal over, MaryAnn carried the dishes to the dishpan on the stove and covered the food on the table with a clean cloth. William John grabbed his hat and walked to the open front door. "Sounds like a horse is coming on the road," he said. He waited until the rider came into view. Then he turned and dashed through the back door, calling over his shoulder, "It's Lee William, riding hard. It must be Lucy's time."

Shaking her head in wonder, MaryAnn spoke out loud to herself. "He'll be at the barn before Lee William makes the front gate. He'll have the horse saddled and be back before I can put on a clean apron."

Ten minutes later, with MaryAnn mounted behind William John, they all rode back to the waiting Lucy.

MaryAnn and William John stayed the night, for little Anna Marie did not arrive until well after dark. MaryAnn searched Lee William's face. "You lookin' for a boy, were you?" she asked gently.

"Might be our twins buried back in Indiana will be the only boys we have, Mama," he answered. "I just look for healthy babies anymore."

Seeing how he beamed at Lucy and the tiny infant lying beside her, MaryAnn allowed that for the time being at least he had quit brooding over the Kansas problems.

Even the birth of a new daughter did not stop Lee William's brooding for long. A week later he quarreled with his father over the Kansas situation.

As was usually the case, the papers from Carrick's Mill had started it. It had been three weeks since William John had gone to the mill and MaryAnn allowed that they had missed a lot of news—most of it bad. Senators in Washington were getting so fired up over slavery that they were beating up on one another. Such a senseless thing—that young bully Brooks breaking his cane over old man Sumner's head. And if that weren't bad enough, there were problems in Lawrence over in the Territory. The slavers had been bound to sack the town, considering that it was the seat of the abolitionists. And they did. Then old John Brown, like the crazy man that people said he was, had murdered five men—hacked them to death—at Pottawatamie Creek.

Lee William read the paper aloud, as he sat in his parents' kitchen. When he was finished, he laid the paper down and looked at his father. Speechless, his deep brown eyes registered both torment and confusion.

William John looked at Lee William sympathetically. "Sounds mighty bad, Son," he said. "Sounds like the whole world's gone crazy, but I'm sure it won't touch us here on Dogwood Creek."

Lee William fairly exploded. "How can anything as wicked and violent as what's going on in Kansas not affect us here? How can it not affect this whole country?" Waving the paper in the air, he demanded, "What's happening, Pa? What kind of crazy world am I bringing our babies into? I've always believed that God Almighty has to be on the side of anyone who hates slavery, but what if the man who hates slavery turns out to be a butchering madman? Whose side is God on then?"

Without giving William John a chance to answer, he threw the paper on the table and stomped out the door.

———

MaryAnn thought about Lee William long into the night. The next morning, sitting across the breakfast table from William John, she decided to speak her mind.

"I think you let our son down last night," she began abruptly. "I know you may not think you have any answers, but you got to try."

His listening gave her courage to continue. "I been thinkin' about somethin', rememberin' you talkin' to my pa in Indiana when we was first married. Papa had nightmares all his life about Indian spears and bloody bodies and burned-out homesteads. Seems like he just couldn't forget that he had been orphaned by Indians and he always thought God was to blame somehow . . . until you talked to him, that is. I can see you now as plain as if it was yesterday—sittin' there in the parlor of the big house with your Bible open on the table. I don't rightly know what you said but I know that my pa found his belief in the Almighty. He never again blamed God for Indian spears and burned-out homesteads. In fact he quit havin' nightmares about it."

MaryAnn paused, wondering at herself for having made such a long speech. Then, seeing that William John was still listening, she went on. "I think Lee William needs to hear from you some of what you told my pa. Like as not he'll worry himself sick if he don't get some answers. He can live with knowin' that Russell and him don't always seem to be on the same side. He can live with knowin' that you don't want to take any sides. But he won't ever know another day's peace so long as he keeps worryin' over what side God is on."

William John sat quietly for a long time. Then he answered, "I don't rightly know why parents of little boys die by Indian spears any more than I know why fathers of big boys die in runaway buggies. For certain, I don't know why a man who fights to free the Negroes will take an axe to the skull of his neighbor.

"I remember telling your father that I couldn't find in God's book where He explains everything that happens to people. But then I told him that I don't think that's so important. What's important is that God makes it very plain in His Book what He wants people to do. And we need to pay more attention to that."

He looked at her intently, peering into her blue-black eyes. "We got no cause to ask God to explain himself, MaryAnn. We got to get ready for the day when God asks us to explain ourselves."

He paused, deep in thought. Then, covering MaryAnn's hand with his own, he continued, "I can talk to Lee William, MaryAnn, but this is different than with your pa. Your pa didn't know anything about the Bible. He needed someone to tell him what God did for Him and how he could trust the Almighty for himself.

"Lee William knows all that already. He has studied the Book for a long time. I know you worry about him, but what Lee William needs most is time to think through what he already knows. He'll be a mite miserable for a while, but you'll see . . . he'll work it out."

Fall came quietly upon Dogwood Creek, painting the woods into a colorful canopy. The first small strokes of scarlet fell on the sumac and sassafras, followed by great splashes of yellow, which covered the ash and hickory. Large stands of oak trees shone bronze in the autumn sun, while here and there clumps of gum or maple accented the picture with their individual shades of red.

Reluctant to miss the season's beauty, MaryAnn hurried about her housework each morning and spent long hours outdoors. She gathered the last of the apples from the hilltop orchard and stored them in the cellar. She searched Solomon's Ridge for hickory nuts and collected hazel nuts from the bushes near the chicken house. She stomped the walnuts that had fallen in the yard, pushing off the green hulls and leaving the nuts to dry under the tree. As the days shortened and the leaves began to fall, she remarked to William John that autumn on Dogwood Creek was almost as appealing as May. "But," she lamented, "fall always seems to rush by and, before you know it, winter's here." She shuddered slightly, showing her usual dread of the coming season.

With fall came the presidential election and William John told MaryAnn that he had fixed his hopes on James Buchanan. He reasoned that the next president would get right in the middle of the Kansas problem, because the Territory was pushing for statehood.

"We need a peacemaker," William John had told Lee William one day as they discussed the coming election. "We need a president who won't take sides." Because Buchanan had been in England during most of the slavery-abolitionist struggles, William John figured him to be the best man for the job.

When the report came that Buchanan had won the November election, William John said they could all breathe easier. Lee William wasn't so sure. "Sooner or later he'll have to decide for or against the slavers, Pa. The question's got to be settled." MaryAnn could see that their son still brooded over the right or wrong of the matter.

The two men followed the papers carefully that winter as the country awaited the inauguration of the new president. William John continued in his optimism that Buchanan would bring peace to Kansas territory, but Lee William stubbornly maintained that he would wait and see.

———————

Four months later, in March of 1857, Russell surprised the family with his first visit. He rode the mail coach to Carrick's Mill and walked from there, carrying the latest newspaper, which included a full account of the recent inauguration. MaryAnn and William John glanced briefly at the front page, but quickly laid it aside in their excitement over seeing their son again. They sat at the table long after supper and listened as Russell talked about his new life in the city.

Later, in their room, MaryAnn said to William John, "I've never seen Russell so talkative . . . or so happy." Searching for the right words, she admitted to her husband that he had been right all along about Russell needing a change. In the darkness, she settled into bed beside William John and mentally scolded herself for not seeing the wisdom of his words sooner. She fell asleep praying that she would learn to trust both the Almighty and her husband more.

It was noon the next day before they looked again at the forgotten newspaper. Lee William, joining his father and brother for dinner, read the account of the inauguration eagerly. Then, coming to an item on the supreme court's Dred Scott decision, he exclaimed, "They're all a bunch of slavers! You can't trust any of them." Turning to his father he said evenly, "Let's just hope Buchanan is stronger than that bunch of judges." William John, looking unperturbed, reminded his son that St. Louis slaves suing their masters for freedom had nothing to do with people on Dogwood Creek.

———————

After Buchanan's March inauguration, Lee William followed every action the president took—or failed to take. Week after week, he brought the newspaper from Carrick's Mill to discuss with William John. The more Lee William read, the less he believed that Buchanan was right for the country.

Through the summer and into the early fall, MaryAnn watched her son chafing over the country's politics. By the time October came again, Buchanan had been in office for seven months, and MaryAnn had begun to wish that the newspapers didn't come to Carrick's Mill. "I'm that tired of Lee William and his pa talkin' about how Buchanan's doin' and whether or not the Kansas problem's gettin' worse," she complained to Lucy. William John and Lee William had gone for supplies in midafternoon, and MaryAnn had walked over to Lucy's cabin to visit while they waited for the men to return.

She sat in Lucy's kitchen, rocking eighteen-month-old Anna Marie. Lucy, swollen with child, busied herself laying out a cold supper. Arial and Amy played near the door, listening all the while for the first sound of wagon wheels rumbling along the road. Arial held a jumping jack toy that Lee William had made. As she worked the handles back and forth, Amy watched intently, giggling each time the little wooden man swung his hinged legs into the air.

It was dark when the men came in, discussing the latest news. Lee William was livid. "The slavers have gone and drafted a constitution at LeCompton that's bound to make Kansas a slave state," he raged. "Everybody knows the majority of Kansans want it to be a free state, but the way they've drafted this, no matter how they vote, they can't outlaw slavery in the Territory." He thumped the paper on the table as he declared, "That document's bound to be as fraudulent as a pregnant mule. We'll see how far they get with it. We'll see what the people say when they vote on it in December. We'll see what Buchanan does if the Territory pushes for statehood with *that* constitution."

With his characteristic calm, William John reminded Lee William that on Dogwood Creek they needn't be concerned about Kansans fighting over constitutions, and then changed the subject. "The papers from St. Louis say this whole country's in a recession," he said. "But we are mighty blessed here. Look at our root cellars. Look at our corn crop this year.

We'll have some left to sell after our winter's supply is stored. Next week we'll run the cane and we're going to have enough molasses for three families. Come winter, we'll butcher a hog. Can't you see—the troubles that come to the rest of the country can't touch us on Dogwood Creek."

Lee William listened respectfully, but said nothing in response. MaryAnn wondered silently whether William John could be exaggerating about Dogwood Creek. She reasoned that no place could be completely free from trouble.

But she could not argue with William John about the success of their homestead. For certain, their cellar held enough for two winters or more. They had all they needed and some to spare. Another two or three years and they would own their land free and clear—that is, if they didn't wear out first.

Looking at William John's deeply lined face, she reasoned that there was at least one problem on Dogwood Creek—too much work and not enough rest. The only time the work ever let up was after the snow came.

Later, riding home in the wagon, she wondered if the first snow might fall very soon. There had been sundogs in the west for the last two days and tonight there was a great circle about the moon. "Looks like an early winter," she said as she drew her wrap closer. "Much as I hate winter, I'll be glad to see it this year. At least you'll get a mite more rest."

"I am tired lately," William John said quietly. "But it's nothing to worry your head about."

His admission startled her. She felt a shiver run down her back. An unexplained fear clutched her heart. Silently, she told herself that it was just the thought of winter coming. But try as she would, she could not stop the sudden dread from settling around her like an extra, unwanted cloak.

CHAPTER TEN

A Winter of the Heart

———— ∾ ————

The first snow fell on All Saints' Eve. It had rained all day from early morning. At noon the wind from the north swept in, and soon the rain turned to a wet slushy snow. By suppertime a thin carpet of snow lay on the ground. As MaryAnn dried and stacked the few dishes from their meal, Lee William called "hello" at the back door. Knowing that he had surely come to fetch them for the birthing, MaryAnn grabbed her cloak and wrapped it tightly around her head and body. In a few minutes she and William John were both ready. By the light of two lanterns they trudged up the hill, single file, through the orchard and the ridge field to Lee William's cabin. MaryAnn, walking between the two men, ducked her head to keep the falling snow from catching in her eyelashes. As the lamplit window of Lee William's cabin came into view, they quickened their pace and soon came to his door.

Hours later, as the light snow continued to fall on Solomon's Ridge, a baby boy was born. Lucy had a difficult time, and MaryAnn and William John were up all night attending her. Lucy and Lee William gazed with delight at their new son. They called him Joseph Jubal for Lucy's pa, and Lucy remarked wistfully, "I'm sorry Pa's not cuttin' near here anymore. Likely he won't see his namesake 'til spring."

Upon looking at her grandson, MaryAnn felt a twinge of worry. *He's a mite small,* she thought, *and his cry's too weak—like he's all worn out somehow.* She forced a smile and said nothing of her fears. *Time enough for that when William John and I are home alone,* she decided.

———————

When daylight came, they returned to their own cabin, making their way slowly through the fresh snow. While it had snowed intermittently all night, it was too wet to pack and it barely covered the path. MaryAnn led the way, consciously slowing her steps as she sensed her husband lagging behind.

Once inside the kitchen, William John slumped into the nearest chair while MaryAnn prepared their breakfast. She made quick work of it, but William John fell asleep before she finished and only woke up when she set a steaming cup of coffee in front of him.

He had hardly swallowed his last bite of biscuits and gravy when he grabbed his coat and hat and announced he was off to set his winter trapline. "The early cold will make better pelts," he called over his shoulder. "This will be a good trapping year."

"Can't it wait, William John?" she asked. "You're tired. You've been up all night. Can't you rest today?"

But the door slammed on her question. She walked to the window to watch her husband slowly making his way toward the woods. "No, I guess it can't," she muttered against the window pane. "You can't admit that your years are catchin' up with you—that your gait's slowin' down like winter molasses. You don't see the lines in your own face, William John." She watched until he had disappeared over the ridge, thinking all the while that her husband appeared to be about as tired as a man could be.

A week later, William John opened the winter term at the schoolhouse but it lasted only three weeks before the fever struck Dogwood Creek. When more than half the pupils came down with the fever, William John closed the school.

MaryAnn urged him to rest more as he waited to reopen the school. It pleased her that he did take more time with his morning chores. And he checked his trapline at a more leisurely pace, taking Lee William along as often as possible. But he worried that there would not be time to finish the winter term after the sickness ran its course—that plowing season would overtake them before they could make up the lost time. And when word came that Mrs. Robin had died of the fever, William John insisted on going over to sit up with the body.

MaryAnn sent fresh-baked bread and a pot of rabbit stew along and waited anxiously for his return the next day. When he came in, cold from the ride and haggard from lack of sleep, she convinced him to go to bed. "Lee William can check the traps," she said. "And I've already done the milkin'." He slept most of the day and through the night. The next morning he looked so rested that MaryAnn imagined the lines in his face were not quite so deep.

———

Then, early in December, William John took the fever.

It came on during the night and he didn't get up for milking the next morning. MaryAnn got up before first light and stirred up the fire in the cookstove. She had biscuits in the oven, coffee boiling, and ham sizzling in the pan before it came to her that William John had not yet gone to the barn.

She went to the bedroom and shook him gently. "William John, you're late with—" Her hand brushed over his brow. Fear hit her, like an iron weight settling in the pit of her stomach. "You're burnin' up," she said anxiously. Then, trying to be calm, "You stay right here. I'll handle the milkin'."

She received no protest. He smiled weakly, closed his eyes and went to sleep again.

———————

Milking over, MaryAnn set her buckets down long enough to close the barn door and then picked them up again, intent on hurrying down the path toward the house. A frown puckered her brow as she wondered anxiously about William John. Deep in thought, she did not see Lee William approaching the barn until he was almost beside her. Startled, she jumped slightly, spilling some of the milk.

She laughed lightly at her clumsiness, then grew sober at once as she looked at Lee William's expression. "From the looks of your face, I'd say you don't bring good news, Son," she said.

"No, Mama." His shoulders sagged as he spoke. "It's Lucy and the baby. They're both down with the fever." He brushed his hand over the stubble on his cheek as he continued. "Fact is, all the kids are sick except Arial. I came to see if you could help us."

"Your pa's in bed, Lee William," MaryAnn replied. "He was too sick to milk. I can't leave him alone. But you come inside and we'll figure out what to do." He smiled halfheartedly, took the milk pails from MaryAnn, and walked down the path beside her.

It took only a few minutes for MaryAnn and Lee William to decide they should all be together. MaryAnn could care for William John, Lucy, and the children, and Lee William could mind the stock, fetch water and wood, and take care of the trapline. While Lee William went to hitch the wagon and collect his family, MaryAnn made up beds in the loft.

By midmorning the sick ones were settled in their beds. Arial, who would soon be six, announced that she would be Grandma MaryAnn's helper. MaryAnn sent her to play on the stairway and told her to listen carefully in case her mama or sisters called for anything.

MaryAnn brewed pennyroyal tea and urged it on each patient. She went from William John's room to the loft several times each hour, feeling foreheads and asking about each one's comfort. She prepared broth and, at supper time, carried it to Lucy and the girls. Her heart felt lighter as she watched them eat, but later when she offered some to William John, he could not eat. After only a spoonful, he fell wearily to his pillow once more. Gently she prodded him to drink more tea, but he refused even that.

She sat long into the night rocking little Joseph, feeling his feverish little head hot against her heart. When he had settled at last, Lee William carried him back to Lucy's bed and fell in beside them. MaryAnn pulled her rocker beside William John's bed and sat beside him until morning, sleeping now and then with her head hanging over her chest.

By the second morning Lucy and the girls began to improve, and by the end of the week they were up and around.

But William John and baby Joseph seemed no better for all MaryAnn's care.

When Lucy was strong enough, she assumed care of her baby son and MaryAnn turned her full attention to William John. Day after day she sat beside his bed, urging him to drink the pennyroyal tea. Helplessly, she watched him— burning with fever and shaking the bed with a great chill that would not go away. She piled quilts on him, but still William John complained of the cold. She heated cornmeal in the oven and poured it into an empty sugar sack. When she had tied the sack tightly, she placed it in the bed next to William John's feet. For two days she kept a pan of meal heating in the oven, changing the sack every half hour. But William John never got warm again.

On a frozen January morning, in 1858, he died.

MaryAnn sat beside his lifeless body, mute and dry-eyed through the morning. She stared at William John's face and wondered at the man he had become in the last years—the years since he tracked his horse to Dogwood Creek. She pondered the winters and springs of their life together and allowed that the beginning of those times had not rightly prepared her for the end.

Through the window she saw the shadows cast by the bleak winter sun, past its midday mark. She stared at the great oak tree, shorn and bereft of its leaves, and wondered how long William John would have lived if he hadn't come to Solomon's Ridge.

It came back to this place, to this isolated Ozark homestead that her husband had imagined the first day he stood under that oak tree. To this land where an older man had to begin like a young one—clearing before he could plow or plant; cutting trees before he could hew the logs or rive the shingles for his house. It came back to his wild dream of having their own land and of being the first teacher on Dogwood Creek. It even came back to Logan Bennett with his idea that William John should hold Sunday meetings in the schoolhouse. Most of all it came back to William John's fool horse, and MaryAnn wished bitterly that the horse had stayed in Indiana.

By and by she was conscious of stirring in the other rooms. But she made no move until Cora Bennett came and gently touched her on the shoulder.

"MaryAnn," Cora spoke softly, "we've come to help lay out the bodies."

Cora's words drifted slowly through the cloud of pain that surrounded MaryAnn. *Bodies?*

"What did you say, Cora?" MaryAnn looked at her friend. "Did you say bodies? Is baby Joseph . . . "

Cora nodded before MaryAnn could speak the word. "I'm right sorry, MaryAnn."

MaryAnn stared, unseeing, for a moment. Then, rising from the chair, she smoothed her apron and walked toward the kitchen with slow, deliberate steps. From a peg behind the cookstove, she drew on her cloak and pulled it tightly around her. "I'll be goin' to pick the bury site," she said to Cora. "I reckon we never figured on where the family bury ground would be."

Logan Bennett came to her and touched her lightly on the shoulder. "We have a suggestion, MaryAnn—that is, if you don't mind." He waited for her response.

"Of course."

"We been wonderin' maybe if you'd like to bury William John by the schoolhouse. We thought we might start a community bury grounds there."

107

MaryAnn nodded thoughtfully. "He would like that . . . William John would like that."

As she rehung her cloak on the peg, Lucy and Lee William came into the room. MaryAnn searched Lucy's pale, tear-streaked face. As their eyes met, Lucy's filled and she ran across the room to throw herself into her mother-in-law's arms. For a long while MaryAnn held the sobbing young woman close. She could find no words to say as she stroked Lucy's blonde hair. Suddenly the memory of her own mother came to her.

Catarina had held MaryAnn at such a time—had stroked MaryAnn's hair away from her forehead and cried with her. MaryAnn could almost hear Catarina crying in her native tongue, "Ach mein kinder, mein kinder, mein kinder." They had wept together when MaryAnn's boys died of the fever. And when they buried the boys beside Catarina's baby, Catarina had gathered her daughter into her arms again and held her as a child.

Remembering her mother, MaryAnn patted Lucy's shoulder and let her weep. At length MaryAnn led her to a chair and washed her face with a warm cloth. Soup had appeared on the stove—from Cora, MaryAnn knew—and MaryAnn brought some to Lucy. "Here, eat this," she said. "You need your strength."

She wished for words, but they would not come, so she drew up a chair beside Lucy and sat throughout the long afternoon.

At nightfall, Old Man Carrick's son came with a wagon, bearing two coffins he had made. Cora took charge of the laying out. She saw that the bodies were washed and dressed in clean clothes and laid side by side in the back bedroom. Neighbors spelled each other, sitting up two nights with the bodies until the frozen earth yielded to the picks and shovels of the grave diggers.

At last, on the second morning, the graves were ready—a great gaping hole for William John and a tiny space for Joseph.

Lee William drove the wagon, carrying the coffins behind the seat where the women huddled together. MaryAnn stared blankly at the barren winter landscape and pondered how the closing of one schoolhouse and the opening of another had led to this day. And she questioned whether the Almighty had let her husband down. For all his hard work, William John had not managed to secure the patent on their homestead. The fine house he had built for MaryAnn stood on indebted land and very soon he would be buried beside an empty schoolhouse. She wondered dully what would happen to the land—the homestead that had represented the greatest desire of William John's heart. *For that matter,* she questioned, *what will happen to the schoolhouse?*

Lee William called the team to a halt near the open graves and tied the reins to a tree. He helped the women down from the wagon and they walked to the schoolhouse together. Inside, a fire roared in the cast-iron stove. Old Man Carrick led them in singing, "Death, What a Solemn Call" and it seemed to MaryAnn that Cassie Miller sang loud enough to be heard in the next county. Logan Bennett stood to pray, but his words were lost to MaryAnn, who still heard Cassie's shrill "death takes the young as well as old, an' in the windin' sheet doth fold."

Outside, the men lowered the coffins into the ground while the onlookers milled quietly about. They rubbed mittened hands together and lowered their heads against the cold until the last spadeful of earth covered the coffins. When it was done, Logan shook hands with Lee William and Cora hugged Lucy and MaryAnn. Lucy wept softly, but MaryAnn stood silent and unmoving.

The neighbors loaded into their wagons to ride back to MaryAnn's house, but still she stood there. She stared at the mound and tried to remember what William John looked like the first time she ever saw him—the day he came riding up to the house with her brother George. That was the day she had decided she must learn to cook. She had managed to learn the basics before they married a year later and William John moved into the big house in Indiana.

Indiana. There was a perfectly good graveyard there, William John—daffodils and all, she thought angrily. *But you— you had to be buried on Dogwood Creek, did you? Or did you figure death wouldn't find you here? I reckon that's it. Most likely you figured nothin' could hurt us here as long as we held our peace. But you forgot, William John. The fever—it comes where the war don't bother and the recession can't reach.* She shivered in the cold, suddenly conscious that she was all alone. Resolutely, she set her jaw, picked up her skirts, and marched away to the waiting wagon.

Two hours later MaryAnn surveyed her neighbors, gathered in the parlor. "I thank you for your help," she said, looking from one visitor to the next. "And now I reckon I got some business to 'tend to. I aim to sell William John's horse tomorrow, unless one of you takes him off my hands today. I'll make you a fair price."

A silence fell across the room as every eye turned first to MaryAnn, then to Lee William. Old Man Carrick coughed. Logan Bennett scraped his feet. At length, Lee William spoke.

"Are you sure, Mama?" he asked. "That's a right good saddle horse."

"Good enough horse, Lee William, but I got no use for him. I reckon I'll be in the market for a work horse or a mule maybe. The team's gettin' old. I need somethin' stronger to plow with," she stated flatly.

Again, she looked at her neighbors, one by one. "You heard my son. That's a right good horse and if any of you be a-needin' one, I'll make you a fair price."

CHAPTER ELEVEN

The Widow Chidester

March, 1858

When plowing time came, Lee William took to the fields with a team of little mules. He reasoned that his mother had been right after all to sell the horse, for one of the old work mares had died and the other was none too strong.

Old Man Carrick proudly rode his new saddle horse bought from MaryAnn, and all of Dogwood Creek talked in hushed tones about William John's widow who had shed not one tear since her husband died.

According to Cassie Miller, the widow Chidester was in a trance—as fearsome a trance as you'd ever want to see. What's more, if you could believe Cassie, some people feared that William John's widow could put a hex on little ones.

The general speculation increased when it was learned that in December Lucy Chidester would give birth to another child. Everyone supposed that it would be a blessing if it were a boy to take the place of baby Joseph—everyone but Cassie Miller, that is. She declared that, boy or girl, Lee William and

Lucy would be mighty blessed if the child were born without a curse on it.

MaryAnn paid little mind to Cassie Miller, whom she considered a meddlesome creature, or to the talk that drifted back to her through Cora Bennett. On the other hand, she did nothing to lay the talk to rest. She was often seen wandering through the woods or standing beside William John's grave, talking in hushed tones.

At home, even when Cora came to call, MaryAnn went about her work methodically, talking very little, smiling not at all, and never shedding a tear. She listened attentively when Cora spoke her fears about a coming war. "I don't like it, MaryAnn," Cora said on a recent afternoon. "The papers say that with all his braggin' about cotton, the senator from South Carolina is practic'ly darin' the northerners to go to war. He said that cotton's king, and nobody better make war against it. What do you make of it, MaryAnn? S'pose there'll be a war?"

MaryAnn responded woodenly, "I don't know, Cora. S'pose if there is, it'll come to Dogwood Creek?" She grew silent then, remembering the many times that William John had said that war would never come to Dogwood Creek. She could almost see his eyes—all serious and fixed on her face, the way he always looked when he made a promise to her. She could hear again the confidence in his voice as he spoke the words, "We're safe here, MaryAnn. Nothing can reach us on Dogwood Creek." Bitterly, she pushed the remembered words from her mind. *You lied to me, William John,* she thought. *You had no right to make me a promise you couldn't keep.*

Cora studied MaryAnn's impassive face and recognized that once more MaryAnn had turned to her brooding. She spoke gently, "MaryAnn?"

MaryAnn looked at her neighbor blankly, then said matter-of-factly, "What were we talkin' about, Cora?"

Ignoring the question, Cora stood up slowly, saying that it was time for her to be going along and wouldn't MaryAnn come to see her soon?

MaryAnn nodded politely but admitted, "I don't get out much, Cora. I don't even go up the hill to Lee William's anymore."

Cora hesitated a moment, a look of pity in her eyes, but she pressed no more.

————————

On an afternoon in late June, as MaryAnn hung the last of the wash, she looked up to see Russell walking through the gate. He crossed the yard with quick, long strides and caught MaryAnn close with his good arm. He had not been to Dogwood Creek since before William John died and he clung to her now as if needing her comfort. MaryAnn felt herself stiffening in his embrace. When he released her, she smoothed her apron awkwardly and said to him, "I'm glad you've come, Son." The words came out crisp and polite and MaryAnn wondered at the emptiness she felt. *A mother ought to feel happy when a son comes to visit,* she thought, *but seems like I don't feel anythin' anymore.*

Concern registered on Russell's face. He looked at her quizzically as he said, "Lee William wrote to me, Mama. He's worried about you. He says all the neighbors are worried."

They brought chairs and sat on the front porch to catch the late afternoon breeze. When they had settled, MaryAnn said, "The neighbors talk too much. They'd oughta be mindin' their own business."

Russell sat quietly for a moment. He cleared his throat nervously and began to massage his withered arm. "I don't mean to pry, Mama, but is it true you haven't even cried?"

"A woman my age gets short on tears, Son. Seems like I don't have any left."

He dropped his hand to his lap and said almost in a whisper, "Mama, I don't believe that. And I don't think it's good for you to tell yourself that. It's not right somehow. A woman just naturally grieves when her husband dies."

"This is not about grievin', Son," she said sharply. "Cryin' and grievin's two different things."

Their eyes met as she spoke and he replied at once, "You're angry, Mama . . . have I offended you?"

"Now what would I have to get angry about?" she asked testily. "I left a good home and a big farm and came to this place because my husband had his heart set on ownin' a piece of land. He always told me that this was a safe place to be, a place where nothin' would touch us. And now he's dead in his grave and I've got this nice house settin' on a quarter section that'll probably never be paid for. What's more, I don't remember gettin' a choice in any of this." She drew a long breath when she had finished.

Russell raised his eyebrows. "I thought you liked it here."

"There's no place on God's earth any prettier than Dogwood Creek," she agreed. "This is not about places—not about Indiana or Missouri." She glanced away from him, fixing her eyes on a squirrel scampering up the walnut tree.

Russell scraped his chair closer to his mother and laid his hand on her arm. "Maybe you could explain what it *is* about."

She shrugged. "It's about old men tryin' to be young again. It's about men goin' after what their hearts want and then dyin' before they've half finished what they set out to do." To herself, she added, *It's about the Almighty lettin' good men down.*

A look of understanding crossed Russell's face. He grasped his mother's arm firmly with his good hand. "Mama, a man is better for having a dream. Even if he never reaches his dream, he's better for having tried it."

"And what of it now, Russell? What happens to your pa's dream now?"

"Pa wanted a place to leave to the next generation, Mama. That was what his heart most desired. But Pa's gone. You have to decide what you want now. Do you want to stay on Dogwood Creek?"

His question surprised her, for she had not thought to ask it of herself. Having been confronted with it, she wondered how to answer. "What do you think I oughta do, Son?" she asked at last.

"I'm not the one to tell you, Mama. In the first place I never would have come to this place. I wouldn't live on Dogwood Creek if I owned the whole section. But you—you seemed to like it well enough. I know at first you didn't really have a choice, but you have one now. If you don't want to stay, then come to St. Louis, or go back to Indiana . . . just don't go on blaming Pa for dying and leaving you here when you could choose to live somewhere else."

MaryAnn listened intently, considering Russell's words. In all the months since William John died, she had not once asked herself if she wanted to leave Dogwood Creek. She had let her anger simmer day by day as she told herself that if it hadn't been for William John, she wouldn't be living in Missouri. It was just like Russell to point out to her that if she were stuck here against her will, she could very well change all that. She knew he wouldn't let it go until she told him straight out what she wanted to do.

As she considered what to say, the question nagged at her. *Would I really want to leave here? And if I stay, how can I go on blamin' William John for a choice I make?* She stood from her chair then and swept her eyes over the landscape—from the little south field past the springhouse to the north hill where the chicken house stood. Silently she acknowledged that it wasn't William John's doings that kept her on Dogwood Creek. Even if Russell were right—even if the choice were hers, she could not imagine leaving this place.

Aloud she said, "I reckon you're right, Son. I could leave here if I wanted." Having said it, she was surprised to find that she felt a little less angry with her dead husband.

———

The question of MaryAnn's choice did not come up again during the two days that Russell stayed. Stubbornly, Mary-Ann refused to declare any decision on the matter, but she felt sure that Russell knew she would never leave Dogwood Creek.

When he returned to St. Louis, he left at midmorning in order to catch the mail coach. MaryAnn stood at the open door watching his disappearing form and then sat down at the kitchen table to read the newspaper he had left behind. She had hardly finished the first item when Cora called, "Hello!" from the porch. Soon the two neighbors were pouring

118

over the paper together, discussing once again the possibility of war.

Cora pointed to a story about a lawyer from Illinois who had been nominated by the Republicans to run against Senator Douglas for the United States Senate. "Look, Mary-Ann," she said, thumping her fist on the table, "if he's not talkin' about war, the sun don't come up in the east."

MaryAnn read it to herself.

> ... in his acceptance of the nomination, Mr. Lincoln said to his fellow party members, "I believe this government cannot endure permanently half slave and half free." Mr. Lincoln reminded the audience that five years have gone by since a policy was initiated with "the avowed object and confident promise of putting an end to slavery agitation." Further, he stated that the "agitation has not only not ceased, but has constantly augmented. In my opinion it will not cease until a crisis shall have been reached and passed. A house divided against itself cannot stand."

MaryAnn bit her lower lip as she lay the paper down. "One thing's for sure, Cora. This Mr. Lincoln don't think the problems are goin' to go away. What does Logan say about it?"

"Logan's sure that if Mr. Lincoln wins the senate seat he'll likely rile things up in Washington. He thinks we oughta get ready for war, only he don't ever say what we're s'posed to do." Cora looked exasperated.

Through the summer months MaryAnn followed the newspaper accounts of the contest between the two Illinois men. The reading always brought William John to mind. She sat on her front porch in the evenings and remembered the nights when he had debated the slavery question with the boys. She wondered what each might say about the latest developments. She speculated that Russell would agree with Lincoln on some points because Russell always argued for preserving the Union. Lee William would never agree that preserving the Union was more important than abolishing slavery. And William John? William John would argue that people should tend to their own business and not get into a war trying to tell others what to do.

He'd say that if we hold our peace we have nothin' to worry about here, MaryAnn recalled, time after time. And then she would argue with the memory. *It's not true. It's just not true.*

As night fell and the jarflies and katydids competed in noisy concert, MaryAnn would clasp her arms across her breast, rock back and forth and try to recall the feel of her husband's arms. But even there, all alone except for the night creatures, she did not cry.

———

The green scum of dog days lay upon the creek as the hot days of August passed. In late September, Lee William brought the news to MaryAnn that Lincoln had lost the election and Senator Douglas had kept his senate seat. "But they're already talking about running Lincoln for president, next election," he said.

MaryAnn could not tell if Lee William agreed with that idea or not. Since his father's death, he had talked very little to her about anything other than crops. Impulsively, she asked, "Do you think he's a good candidate, Son?"

"Well, from what he says I think he's a lot more concerned about saving the Union than freeing the slaves. I've always wished we could do both. Now Russell, he'll sure vote for Mr. Lincoln. But I reckon I'll wait and see."

When he made no further comment, MaryAnn changed the subject. "How's Lucy feelin'?" she asked.

"She's a mite puny today, but mostly she does all right. She's not been the same since little Joseph died. She still cries over him sometimes."

MaryAnn stared out the window for a long while before speaking. "Let her cry, Son, let her cry," she said.

He looked at her thoughtfully. "Yes, Mama," he answered, "I expect she needs to." Searching her face as he spoke, he pleaded, "Come home with me, Mama. Spend the night. It'll be good for you. It'll be good for Lucy."

She almost protested, but changed her mind. "I'd be pleased," she said. "Just let me get a few things."

She went to her bedroom and laid out a clean nightgown on the bed. She placed her hairbrush and bone comb and such few other things as she needed on top of the gown and then rolled it tightly. Last of all she wrapped a clean apron around it all and tied it into a bundle. She checked her image in the mirror and smoothed her hair before rejoining Lee William.

Ten minutes later they walked up the hill to the orchard and across the field. As Lee William's cabin came into view they saw Arial and Amy playing under the elm tree near the front door with little Anna Marie. Lucy sat in the doorway watching.

The scene made MaryAnn smile. "You've got three mighty sweet girls, Lee William," she said.

"I know," he replied. "And we've had three mighty fine little boys, but . . . seems like we can't keep them."

121

"Maybe Lucy will have another son." MaryAnn tucked her hand through Lee William's arm and gave him a comforting squeeze. She thought about her own father—about how close he and George had always been; and how when her bachelor brother died, her father's name would also die; about how she had given her family name to Russell so that if there were to be no more Breans, at least there was Russell Brean Chidester. Again she squeezed Lee William's arm as she said, "I know a man wants a son to carry his name."

"We'd like that, Mama," he agreed. "But it'd go mighty hard with Lucy to have to bury another boy. I just want a strong healthy child."

MaryAnn had no time to answer, for Arial looked up to see them coming and ran down the little rise to meet them. With her dark eyes and bouncy brown curls, she resembled her father when he was small. Chubby, blond-haired Amy followed close behind. They splashed through the little creek that ran along the bottom of the property and threw their arms around MaryAnn's legs. She leaned down to kiss them, smiling at their pleasure in seeing her.

Lee William jumped across the stream just in time to grab Anna Marie who was tumbling down the rise after her sisters. She too had Lee William's coloring, but when she smiled, everyone said she looked like Lucy. Lee William picked the child up in one arm and reached for MaryAnn's bundle. "I'd best take that, Mama. You'll need a hand for each girl." Then, laughing as they went, they trooped to the cabin, where Lucy waited at the door.

"This purely is a surprise," Lucy greeted her mother-in-law. "I'm glad you've come."

MaryAnn enjoyed the visit so much that, within a few hours of her arrival, she promised the girls that she would come again soon. As she tucked them into bed that night, she helped them count on their fingers the days until she would be back again.

Back in the kitchen with Lee William and Lucy, MaryAnn was plainly annoyed to learn that Cassie Miller had taken to dropping by Lucy's every time the Millers went to Carrick's Mill.

"She's all the time askin' kin she do anythin' fer me," Lucy explained. "I allus tell her, 'Thankee kindly, but Lee William's mama is that good to help.' But it don't seem to make no difference. She jist keeps a-comin'. She's bent on bein' here for the birthin'."

"But she can't believe that she's needed," MaryAnn protested. She stood in the middle of the room, hand on hip. "I'll be here to help you. I've done it so often with William John. We don't need Cassie's help."

"I tole her that, ma'am, but she don't pay me no mind."

"Well, we'll just have to make it plain to her," replied MaryAnn. "I don't like the thought of that nosy old woman bein' around when the next Chidester baby comes into the world."

CHAPTER TWELVE

Little John

———— ❧ ————

The fall passed into December and MaryAnn resigned herself to staying inside for the season of cold. The first snow came late and soon disappeared, leaving the landscape bare and ugly. MaryAnn avoided looking out the windows, for she hated the sight of naked trees. She huddled near the cookstove, recalling the previous December. The memory of William John's death emerged before her, day and night. At night she piled on extra quilts to make up for the lack of his warm body next to hers. During the day she pondered over the fact that while extra quilts took the chill from her bed, nothing seemed to take it from deep inside her breast.

Even in bleak December, MaryAnn knew that her mind was made up—she would never leave Dogwood Creek. Strangely she felt no satisfaction in the decision, and she felt no optimism about the future. She sought comfort from William John's Bible but almost always laid it aside after a few minutes. She could not help herself—she felt that Almighty God had let William John down. And having decided that, she couldn't bring herself to listen to what such a God had to say.

On the tenth day of December, MaryAnn packed a few things and tramped over the hill to Lee William's cabin. "I best stay now until your time comes," she told Lucy. "You never can tell when we might get more snow."

Lee William pointedly told the Millers that MaryAnn was staying with them, but it didn't keep Cassie from checking on Lucy. She happened by on the very morning Lucy's birth pains began. Logan and Cora had brought their wagon across the ridge to fetch the girls. Cassie came just as they were leaving. Cora, sensing MaryAnn's feelings, tried to persuade Cassie to come home with her and entertain the children. But Cassie insisted on staying. "It's my neighborly duty," she argued.

Determined to ignore Cassie, MaryAnn went on with her preparations. She brought extra padding for Lucy's bed and a basin for catching the afterbirth. She laid clean scissors and string nearby for handling the cord. Lucy herself had readied the cradle and laid out a small piece of blanket for wrapping the baby.

Cassie followed MaryAnn around, making suggestions and dire warnings about the birth process. Irked at the interruption, MaryAnn wondered how to best handle the situation. Drawing a deep breath, she pulled up a chair in the far corner. "I'm forgetting my manners, Cassie," she said with exaggerated politeness. "Why don't you have a chair right here? That way, if we need anything, we can call you easy." She looked unflinchingly into Cassie's eyes as she spoke. Cassie quickly turned her head aside as though to avoid looking into MaryAnn's eyes. Meekly she backed into the chair and sat down.

Returning to the bedside, MaryAnn rubbed Lucy's arm comfortingly as the younger woman cried out in pain. She felt Cassie staring at her and deliberately turned to gaze into Cassie's eyes once more. Again Cassie jerked her head aside.

Silently MaryAnn pondered the other woman's strange behavior. *She really believes I could put a hex on someone. She's afraid I'll put one on her.* In a moment of insight, MaryAnn devised a plan. If need be, she would simply stare into Cassie's eyes—that would keep the woman at a safe distance! She recalled the tales that Cassie had started during the past year and wondered what new story she would concoct for the people of Dogwood Creek.

Outside the bedroom door, Lee William paced the floor and prayed to Almighty God for a healthy baby. Then he prayed for Lucy, that nothing would go wrong, and finally for his mama. He didn't worry that MaryAnn would have any problems doing the birthing without his pa. He worried because his mama had not been herself for almost a year. And he prayed that somehow God Almighty would help her. Once again he heard the sudden cry of pain and saw by the mantel clock that two hours had gone by. He prayed that it would not be long.

In the bedroom Lucy winced and held MaryAnn's arm as she bore down on the pain. Her face flushed with the effort, and when it was over, she lay back, panting for breath. MaryAnn checked the progress and smiled at her daughter-in-law encouragingly. "You're doing fine," she said. "It won't be long now."

127

As Lucy's pains came closer, MaryAnn concentrated on helping her and forgot that Cassie sat across the room. She thought fleetingly of William John and how this was the first time she had attended a birthing without him. She wiped Lucy's brow and held her hand tightly through one last contraction.

"I reckon you have another son, Lucy," MaryAnn announced, smiling at her daughter-in-law.

Lucy looked radiant as she watched MaryAnn clean and wrap the baby. "This baby—he's the seventh child," she said. "Lee William and me—we decided that iffen it wuz a boy, his rightful name would be William John the Second, after his grandpa Chidester. But if it be the same to you, we'll call him Little John."

MaryAnn's eyes widened with surprise. To think that William John should have a grandson named for him brought a lump to her throat. Suddenly it came to her—this was what William John's dream was all about. He wanted to provide for his sons and their sons after them. She had thought it selfish and impulsive of him to uproot her. She had blamed that fool horse as if the poor animal had chosen to be taken from the barn and led off to Missouri. And she had blamed William John for using the horse as a thin excuse to run away from what was comfortable and secure and go chasing after some new excitement. Not once had she considered the possibility that William John had given careful thought to his dream and to what it would take to pursue it. She had never recognized that he also had given up comforts and had worked well beyond his strength so that he might leave something of himself behind.

As she stood holding her husband's namesake, her bitterness began to melt away. She looked at the child and saw the reason for William John's coming to Missouri. More than that, she saw in the face of the infant her own reason for staying on Dogwood Creek.

She mulled over Lucy's words. The child would bear her husband's name, but Little John would also be a special part of her. After all, they were both seventh children.

MaryAnn sucked in her breath. A tear rolled down her cheek. Then another. She clasped the baby to her breast and began to rock back and forth while she stood. Soon her tears gave way to great racking sobs.

Lee William came rushing into the room, a look of alarm on his face. He stopped directly in front of his mother, then turned to Lucy, an unspoken question on his lips.

"It be alright," she said gently. "We have another son."

Lee William turned to his mother again. "Can I see him now, Mama?" he asked. But MaryAnn continued to rock back and forth, the tears falling freely, her hands locked around the infant. Gently Lee William pried her fingers loose and took his son from MaryAnn's arms. Tenderly he lay the child beside Lucy on the bed and, together, they bent over him, examining every feature of the tiny head.

After a moment, Lee William stood again and walked to his mother who was still sobbing uncontrollably. He wrapped her in his arms and said, "Go ahead and cry, Mama. It's time." She clung to him as her sobs subsided.

When she had grown quiet, she wiped her tears on the corner of her apron and pushed back a stray wisp of hair from her face. She walked over to the bed and stooped to kiss the baby on the forehead. "Seventh child, indeed," she whispered. "You are the seventh child of the seventh son of the seventh child." And then in a barely audible whisper she spoke to the child. "Maybe for you, we can carve out this farm just like your grandpa wanted. Maybe for you, we can do it." She raised herself up straight, smiled at Lee William, and said, "May the Almighty make it so. May God make it so."

Across the room in the corner, Cassie Miller watched with widened eyes and gaping mouth.

———

Before three days passed, all of Dogwood Creek knew that William John Chidester had a new namesake. What's more, if you could believe Cassie Miller, his widow had been cured of her trance. "I seen it with my own eyes," Cassie declared up and down the creek. "Her what never cried a tear when her husband died, cried a bucket or more when that child wuz born. I declare she held that baby so hard that I wuz afeared she wud smother him. She tried to croon to it but the only thing what come out was turrible moans—a sure sign that the trance wuz beginnin' to break. Lee William, he come a runnin' in, his face pale as ashes. I knowed he wuz a thinkin' the baby wuz dead. After he tuk the child and laid it in Lucy's arms, the widder, she reached over and kissed the baby on the forehead and whispered somethin' kinda strange-like. When she looked up I knowed she wuz cured of the trance."

Try as they would, no one could pry from Cassie Miller the words that MaryAnn Chidester had spoken to the baby. "Won't do fer me to go repeatin' that," she declared. "Mought bring back the trance iffen I did."

The truth was, Cassie could not tell because she had not heard what MaryAnn had whispered.

A week after the birth, MaryAnn sat alone at her kitchen table eating her breakfast of hot mush. Outside, a cold dry snow had begun to fall. Seeing it, MaryAnn left her half-eaten breakfast and went to the window. She stood quietly watching, feeling a strange attraction to the softly falling snow. "You remember I always hated winter, William John," she whispered. "But today, the snow puts me in mind of the Almighty—like He's coverin' all the ugliness with a blanket of white. Puts me in mind of new beginnin's. You were right, William John. God's not to blame for runaway wagons or fevers or half-finished dreams. I've been a stubborn old woman ever since you went away, William John. I've been blamin' you for lettin' me down and I've been blamin' the Almighty for lettin' you down. I'm not sure you had ever'thin' right about Dogwood Creek, but I can see now you were always right about one thing. Almighty God won't ever forsake us. He's been mighty patient with me—never turned His back on me even when I was tryin' to turn mine on Him.

"You were right about somethin' else, William John. This place is where the Chidesters belong. I don't know how we'll do it, but I aim to see your dream come true." She paused in her pondering and acknowledged, "Only now, it's *my* dream." Her eyes swept over the yard from the walnut tree down to the spring, and she thought of that May day when she had first seen this spot. "You have a namesake now, William John, and someday this will all be his," she whispered softly.

She turned from the window and walked to the parlor. She sat down at the library table where she kept William John's Bible. She drew out a pencil from the drawer and opened the Bible to the family records section. For a moment she paused, reading the last two entries in the death column. Then, licking the pencil first, she wrote in the birth column, "William John Chidester, II. December 15, 1858." She surveyed it thoughtfully for a moment and then added, "The seventh child of the seventh son of the seventh child."

Joy Pennock Gage was born in the Missouri Ozarks. She and her husband Ken spent five years in rural mission work, two of which were in a logging camp. They have ministered together in churches in California, Oregon, and Arizona. Joy is the author of numerous books, including *Is There Life After Johnny?* and *Every Woman's Privilege*. She currently lives in San Rafael, California. Joy's father, B.F. Pennock, *is* the seventh child of the seventh son of the seventh child, and she did have a great-grandmother named MaryAnn.